LOVE BITES AND OTHER STORIES

Love Bites

and Other Stories

John B. Keane

THE MERCIER PRESS

The Mercier Press, 4 Bridge Street, Cork
24 Lower Abbey Street, Dublin 1

© John B. Keane 1991

ISBN 0 85342 968 5

A CIP record for this book is available from the British
Library

Printed in Ireland by Colour Books Ltd.

Contents

Love Bites

'THERE ARE some,' said a thirty cow farmer from Moyvane to the north of Listowel, 'who don't hold with breast-feeding in public.'

Earlier that day he had seen a woman breast-feeding a child in a grocery shop.

'Tell that to the child,' said a Ballylongford farmer of lesser stock. The talk had been drifting toward nature all day, not that kind of nature which is under threat from pollution and man-made development but rather the kind that has to do with humanity and it was thus that the conversation turned towards the common or garden love bite. I hold no mandate for love-biting nor do I disapprove. In the wrong hands however it can be damaging to the physiognomy.

Another factor which is not in its favour is that it is not a native pursuit. You might say that it comes under the heading of foreign games although I've never heard of it being banned.

Don't ask me where love-biting originated. I suggest that the first nibble was taken in Italy but I could be wrong. However there may be some enlightened reader who might be able to provide the answer. It may well have been Morocco. Something tells me that it all began on the shores of the Mediterranean although I once remember reading a survival story set in the remote headwaters of the Amazon. It's hard to refute a tale from there. There was an account of a tribe called the Lottidari. Apparently they specialised in love-biting but it may well have been introduced to these ignorant savages by some member of the so-called civilised

7

world. A missionary to whom I once spoke told me that it might well be a substitute for cannibalism, the relict of some ancient tribe who had partaken too much of each other.

'Breast-feeding,' said the thirty cow farmer from Moyvane, 'is a healthy practice because children that are breast-fed are full of nature and them that gets their diet out of cans has no nature at all and that's what's wrong with the world today.'

I had heard this hairy old canard before. In fact if ever hairy old canards start going bald this will be one of the first to do so.

'I'll tell ye all something now,' said the twelve cow farmer from the Stacks Mountains, 'and you wouldn't catch me saying it unless it was true.'

This was a rare submission from a man who was never known to have issued a single word of the truth in his life. However hope springs eternal and this might very well be the first time. We waited with bated breaths and after they had been unbated there was no sound save the gentle lapping of stout, beer and whiskey against the rims of glasses great and small. There is no lakewater or sea water or no rippling cadence as unique as the lapping of intoxicating liquor in a glass held by human hands. One has only to recall the sad lines of the exile as he recalls:

Whether I am in Alaska or high in Mandahar
I hear the porter lapping in Mick McCarthy's bar.

What evocative and original lines! Let us hope that the poet who composed them did not die from thirst.

Meanwhile the Stacks' Mountain man was composing himself rather than hurry the eagerly awaited announcement. Eventually he cleared his throat, a task made easy because of the many draughts of liquor assimilated that day. Said he with a baleful eye and a voice rendered mellifluous by alcohol 'there is no nature in a love-bite from false teeth.'

If ever an inflammatory remark was unleashed inside a public bar this was surely it. All the occupants, a brown and white sheepdog apart, were folk of advanced years. One might safely presume that the majority were possessed of false teeth.

Wise old codger that he was the man who passed the derogatory remark made his way towards the front door and, prior to departing, opened his gob to reveal a mouthful of fine natural teeth.

Hatching

I REMEMBER once there was a somewhat contrary hatching hen appointed to sit on a clutch of eggs which weren't her own. She was a Sussex Blue and the eggs were laid by a Rhode Island Red. Maybe this was why she was so reluctant to stay sitting on the eggs. Did hens have a way of knowing one egg from another? I suspect they did.

Certain hens will hatch anything from pheasant to duck eggs but there are no two birds alike as the cock said to the drake. Let us return, however, to our own bird and her reluctance to hatch the eggs of a stranger. There she would settle trancelike as only hens can when suddenly, for no apparent reason, she would make for the door. She would be recaptured instantly and reminded firmly of her obligations but no sooner would she be re-seated than she would desert once more. She exasperated the entire household whose every member took a turn keeping an eye on her.

'There's only one cure for the 'hoor,' announced an old woman who chanced to call one evening for the loan of a cup of sugar.

'What's that?' we all asked.

'The bottle,' said she. We waited for elaboration but none came. We asked again.

'What bottle,' said she, 'but the hot stuff.'

Of course we all knew what the hot stuff was. Weren't the man of the house and his cronies greatly addicted to it without any great harm!

'It will rest the creature,' said the old woman, 'and it will keep her off her feet.'

Up in the 'Room' was a bottle of the very hot stuff in question, as hot, according to himself, as ever was brewed.

'Mix it,' said the old woman, 'with a saucer of Indian meal and you'll end up with a nice paste that she'll find palatable.'

The reluctant hatcher was presented with a saucer of hoochpaste but showed no interest at first. It didn't look very appetising so the woman of the house spoon-fed her till she began to cluck appreciatively and cock her head high for more. I never saw any creature of the female gender take so quickly to booze. In less than three minutes the saucer was empty and she was sleeping as soundly as a drunken apostate during a long sermon.

'She'll die surely,' said the woman of the house.

'She won't nor die,' said himself who knew from long experience that a person could be dead drunk without being dead. How right he was! She slept for several hours without moving, contributing throughout every moment of her repose to the hatching process beneath her craw. When she awakened she tried to rise but failed. She fell asleep again. The next awakening was different. She staggered around the kitchen until she arrived at the door where she was assailed by the arch-enemy of all forms of drunkenness, fresh air. It revived her instantly but a second saucer of hoochmeal was prepared and presented to her before she could sober up. Afterwards she fell asleep for a whole day.

After a fortnight the eggs were hatched and there emerged twelve of the handsomest chicks you ever saw.

The hatcher died soon afterwards of liver disease but she had nobly served her purpose and if some may crib about forcing her into alcoholism I say to these to come and have a gander at the lovely chicks she hatched. They grew up into outstanding specimens of their breed, seven hens and five cocks. One hen who wandered too far from the fowl-run was carried off by a fox but the other eleven survived and I know for a gospel fact that not a solitary one of that fine clutch ever put a taste of booze to their beaks to the day they departed for that heavenly henhouse in the sky. So we see some more of the good uses to which whiskey may be put as if there weren't enough already.

Humble Pie

WISE MEN will tell you that we benefit from suffering, setbacks and letdowns. It's the same with eating humble pie. A man who hasn't been made to eat humble pie has had a diet without roughage.

I would look upon the eating of humble pie as a major developing factor in the human character. My first dosage was administered when I was a schoolboy. I became involved in a fight with a chap who happened to be in the same grade as myself. There the resemblance ended for he was smaller than I was, thinner than I was and as unlikely a candidate for a bout of fisticuffs as a man with two broken hands. Confident of success I indulged in a preliminary bout of shadow boxing prior to the victim's demolition.

A number of other schoolboys had gathered rubbing their hands with delight as is the wont of such characters when mayhem is on the horizon. Alas for me, gathered with them — but unseen by me — was my adversary's brother. I should have known that one or more of his big brothers would have to be in the vicinity. The prospect of being allowed to provide a dazzling exhibition before a live audience had also dazzled my perception.

No sooner had I split the surrounding air with a series of textbook straight lefts than the big brother intervened and informed me that he was about to commence with my maceration. He was the very antithesis of his fraternal inferior with a barrel chest, a jaw like a hippopotamus and a right hand about the same size as a leg of mature lamb.

'Come on!' he shouted truculently as he extended a turnip-sized left hand towards my hitherto unblemished physiognomy.

I did what any intelligent gorsoon would do under the

circumstances especially a gorsoon who aspired to a long and relatively happy life in this vale of tears. I thrust my allegorical tail firmly between my retreating legs and made vague references to a promise I had made my mother whereby I would maintain a peaceful attitude towards all-comers whilst on my way from school.

It was a hollow excuse but I had to try something if I was to extricate myself with some modicum of honour. I was indeed made to eat humble pie on that occasion but the digestion thereof stood me in good stead for the remainder of my school going days. I always looked around for big brothers and other allies when the chips were down.

My final intake of humble pie occurred at a dance some years afterwards. There I was in a new navy-blue suit, in my twenty-first year with legitimate coin of the realm in my trousers pocket and a line of fanciful patter specially designed to woo and ravish consenting females in the vicinity.

Dances came and went and then I saw her sitting on her own in an isolated corner. She was red-haired and vivacious. She was to me what an unexpected oasis is to the parched nomad, what the sight of the sea was to the Greeks of Xenophon when they thought they might never see it again and when they ran towards it shouting 'Thalatta! Thalatta!' I didn't shout thus but I bore down upon the creature like a sheik on an Arabian stallion.

We waltzed to the strains of the Blue Danube. Did I say waltzed? My apologies. We floated but as we were aloft my shoulder was touched by some strange mechanism from the external world. I opened my eyes to find myself confronted by a burly Lothario with a thin moustache so delicately represented that it might have been drawn by a single stroke of a ballpoint pen.

'What's the idea?' I asked.

'The idea,' said he, 'is that this is an excuse-me dance so hand her over.'

I looked to my angelic partner in the hope that she would confirm that it was not an excuse-me but no sound escaped her cherry-coloured lips. Suddenly they were gone and I was alone. I might have eaten humble pie on that occasion but I learned from the experience and ever after when an external object touched me on the shoulder during a dance I whisked my partner to the furthest extremities of the dance-hall where I looked into her eyes and overcame her protestations with flurries of exquisitely executed quicksteps.

The Girls Who Came with the Band

LONG AGO when I first started to dance in country halls I was quite taken by the girls who came with the bands. They would always be dressed more brightly and more fashionably than the local girls and made up to the point of what was regarded as immodest.

Many missioners and priests of the time were death down on paint and powder for reasons best known to themselves but bad as were paint and powder the worst of all was when a girl painted her toenails and wore sandals to flaunt her scarlet toes before the young men of the countryside. Nearly all the girls who came with the bands painted their toes and they wore high-heeled shoes. They also wore short skirts and they didn't care. They were lovely and stylish and beautiful in the eyes of the young men of the hills and the valleys but who were they, these girls who came with the bands?

They weren't vocalists or instrumentalists or they weren't professional dancers hired by the management to lead the floor with a willing partner drawn from the ranks of the locals. They certainly weren't ladies of easy virtue and they weren't the wives or sweethearts of the members of the band.

I had better tell you what they were. They were big-town girls or city girls who had come along with the band for the drive or for the crack. They had grown tired of the fierce competition in the populous halls of the towns and cities. In their own halls they were nobodies but when they came to the village halls and the crossroads halls, they were somebodies. They came armed with the latest steps, the latest hairstyles and they had no real competition

16

from the modest and cautious girls of the locality. Knowing this gave them extra confidence and poise and they took the country halls by storm. In fact any time a really smart girl appeared it was always assumed that she had come with the band.

Only the more daring young men would take them on in the dance — students and lads home from England or soldiers on leave. The girls who came with the bands truly excelled at the tango, their long legs unhindered, freed from all constraints by the excessively long splits in their skirts. The local girls wore the tiniest of splits in their skirts and were inhibited in their movement as a result.

Sometimes the more rustic, the more demure and bashful of the local couples would withdraw from the floor when the lady who came with the band and her partner swept round the hall like a tornado. The newcomers had other important characteristics. They never carried their purses with them when they danced as did the local girls. They left them instead on the stage near the drummer where there was plenty of room and where they were at all times visible although at that time purse-stealing was as rare as the swallowtail coat is now. The fact that they did not carry their purses while they danced meant that they were not available for transportation to areas outside the hall by would-be Romeos. It meant that they had come only to dance and that they had no intention of making up with any male of the area no matter how handsome or how imposing he might be.

Sometimes when a partner swept them to the back of the hall where stood the shy and the halt and the blackguardly these last would pinch them in passing to see if they felt the same as the local girls. These pinches hurt like hell. Once I remember a girl complained to the saxophone player that she had been molested. He laid aside his instrument and left the stage. The girl pointed out the molester and the saxophone player kicked him smartly between the thighs. He sat out the remainder of the dances and all were agreed that he deserved what he got. There is no lower form of animal life than he who would molest a girl.

The girls who came with the band vanished forever shortly after the war. The country girls started to cotton on and soon they began to look themselves like girls who came with the bands.

Insomnia

A WORD or two about insomnia — that scourge that has divided homes and shattered more nerves than all the income tax assessment forms ever wrongfully designed.

There is not a single, solitary soul reading this treatise who has not suffered at some time or other from the scourge of insomnia. Imagine then what it is like to be a chronic insomniac, to know not what the sleep of the just is, to know not what it is to savour sweet slumber when the day's toil is over.

The trouble is that people have forgotten a very important thing about sleep. First of all it's very difficult to locate when you really want it. The thing with sleep is that you must pretend you could not care less about it. That way sleep will come to you but if you persist in hot pursuit you will never catch up with it.

Some wag once said that you would never find a woman or a policeman whenever you really want one. The same thing applies to sleep.

Another thing to remember about sleep is this: it's not to be savoured like a woman. When sleep comes take it at once or you may well have to do without it. You should remember that it's not the sleep itself you enjoy. How could you when you're not conscious? What you enjoy is that brief period before you go to sleep and, of course, that longer period in the morning when you don't want to get up.

When sleep makes its opening bid be sure to take it at once. It will not bid a second time in a hurry and you may be left waiting a long time. That's how insomniacs are made. Don't muck around with your sleep. Sleep is a very tricky business, best defined as a cross between lightning and quicksilver. When confronted with insomnia the thing to do is to really concentrate on staying awake. That way sleep will come in good time.

Insomnia is no fun. I am not trying to make light of it. Why should I? I know not the hour nor the minute that it will lay hold of me.

When I was a gorsoon in Renagown in the Stacks Mountains there was no such thing as insomnia. I'll grant you that a man or a woman might stay awake occasionally thinking of a distant sweetheart but that wasn't insomnia. That was a form of sleeplessness which could easily be cured by joining forces with the missing party. The farmers of the Stack Mountains when I was a boy blamed insomnia in their labourers exclusively on books.

'Books,' they would say, 'are the sworn enemies of sleep.' But this could have been because farmers' 'boys' who had a habit of reading books late into the night were unable to get up in the morning and a farmer's 'boy' who could not get up in the morning was worse than a hen that could not lay an egg.

The reason why there was no insomnia in the Stacks Mountains when I was a gorsoon was that feather ticks were the order of the day. Let me tell you now, those of you who have never slept on a tick of green goose feathers do not know what sweet sleep is like or what it is to dream the sweeter dreams. A tick of green goose feathers transported a man straightaway to the sublime climes of slumberland.

Pills and potions won't cure insomnia. They'll satisfy it for a while and make it hungry for more but they won't dismiss it for good.

Diphtheria came and went in the Stacks as did scarlatina which sounds like a ballet dancer but danced on human life instead. We were exposed to everything except insomnia but now that the feather beds have vanished there is talk of this newfangled sleeplessness in places where it was never heard before.

Circus Passion

THIS IS the story of Antonio Feckawlo often mentioned in passing but never given the full treatment he so richly deserves. Feckawlo was drowned in the Feale River in 1912. Originally of Italian extraction he was, in his heyday, a devil-may-care, curly-haired, moustached Lothario who earned his living as a knife-thrower with Hanratty's Circus which used to tour rural Ireland on a regular basis up until the end of the first world war. As a knife thrower he left a lot to be desired. In straight throws he was quite without peer but in the backhand flip it was rumoured that he wounded several of his human targets.

The reason I am writing about him is that it is over seventy-five years since his body was discovered in the River Feale with a knife clenched between his teeth, his oily hair slicked back without a rib out of place and his dark eyes concentrated in a deathly stare.

Hanratty's Circus consisted of three piebald horses, an aged Shetland pony, a toothless lion who survived on minced donkey meat, a female slackwire walker, the afore-mentioned Antonio Feckawlo and Hanratty himself who quadrupled as lion-tamer, clown, juggler and horse rider. Hanratty's wife saw to the box office.

The trouble started after the night-time performance in Listowel's market place in the year 1910. For some time Hanratty had suspected that his wife had been having a passionate affair with the knife thrower and in this respect his suspicions were to be proved correct. According to residents of Market Street and Covent Lane which still front the market-place Mrs Hanratty, Dolly to her friends, was a red-haired, vivacious lady of fifty odd years where-as Hanratty was thirty years her senior and it might be supposed that the demands of his numerous roles in the ring seriously militated against his prospects as a lovemaker.

The opposite would seem to have been the case with Antonio Feckawlo. Knife-throwing is an artistic vocation calling for little or no physical input. Consequently Feckawlo found himself with considerable time on his hands. Idleness, we are told, makes a mockery of morals. Idleness too, it might be said, is the chief nourishment of lust. Inevitably the knife-thrower and Dolly Hanratty were thrown together and as time passed they grew careless.

In Abbeyfeale one quiet Sunday afternoon, after a matinée, blows were exchanged between Hanratty and the knife-thrower after the former had surprised his wife and her lover as they paddled among the reeds a mile or so upriver from the town. Feckawlo, who was without his knives at the time, was no match for Hanratty who despite his years was still a skilled boxer. Some said he had been a sparring partner with the late Jack Johnson. The upshot of the ruction was that Feckawlo ended up with two black eyes and one broken nose. He fled the scene but, like a true performer, he reappeared for the night performance.

Then came the incident at Listowel, an incident remembered by several octo and nonogenerians mostly female whose eyes still sparkle when they recall the seductive charms of Antonio Feckawlo.

As soon as the later performance ended the taking down of the canvas commenced. This was an event in which all hands, male and female participated. Halfway through the proceedings it was discovered that Dolly Hanratty and Antonio Feckawlo were missing. Immediately Hanratty instituted a search and to his astonishment found the lovers in a warm embrace in the lion's cage.

They foolishly presumed they would be safe from prying eyes in such surroundings. The lion, sated with minced donkey meat, slept soundly as was his wont after late performances.

On this occasion Feckawlo was armed with a wicked-looking knife. Hanratty fled for his life with the Italian at his heels. Hanratty mounted the fleetest of his piebald horses and rode bareback through the streets of the town until he came to the river's edge. Here he dismounted, patted the horse on the rump and hid behind a thorn bush. The horse crossed the swollen river with Feckawlo furiously following.

Thus ends this torrid tale and thus ended the tempestuous career of Antonio Feckawlo at the bottom of the Feale River with his knife still in his mouth. He never knew the river was in flood. As they say in Latin, the language of Feckawlo's ancestors, *nec scire fas est omnia*. It is not permitted to know all things.

Window-Peeping

IF YOU are a peeper-out-of-windows at night please read on. I would improve your lot, not criticise it. If you are interested in establishing the truth regarding the movements of passers-by after the witching hour you should not rely solely upon your own vision.

For instance let us suppose that a man staggers all over the place as he passes by your window it does not mean that he staggers as he passes every window and he may not indeed be the drunkard you think he is. The stagger may have been precipitated by an effort to avoid a dangerous hazard such as a banana skin and as so often happens the manoeuvre may have gotten out of hand because the hazard was not expected. Now if the window-peeper had consulted with other window-peepers up and down the street it might emerge that only one stagger was involved and that far from being intoxicated the after-midnight meanderer was as sober as the window-peeper.

The need for collaborators to determine the truth about the movements of witching-hour wanderers is most pressing. A discreet advertisement placed in one's local paper or in the neighbourhood newsagent's window calling for the assistance of interested window-peepers to monitor the movements of late night revellers and others could well bring the desired results and bring together a team which might monitor the passage of the aforementioned revellers from one end of a given thoroughfare to the other in so comprehensive a fashion that any and all members of the team could testify under oath in a court of law that such a person had gone home rotten drunk on such a night and that another person had gone home sober as the judge who happened to be presiding over the court in question.

Some uncharitable readers are certain to ask what business it is of window-peepers at what hour or in what state a man goes home at night.

The truth is that any person out of doors after midnight is everybody's business. Who is to say but that it is not a burglar on the prowl or it might well be a mugger intent on mischief. None of us should be free from the scrutiny of window-peepers but we are also entitled to fair play in the sense that we would be expecting a truthful and accurate account of our movements.

I have often found a pair of eyes monitoring my midnight movements from certain windows. I happen to know also that the owners of the orbs in question have long since convinced themselves that a man of my ilk would not be abroad after midnight unless he was coming from or going to a drinking session. Reports keep coming in from unsolicited sources suggesting that because of my previous character I could not possibly be engaged in any form of philanthropic mission, that alcohol and alcohol alone had to be the basis for any late night excursion in which I might be involved.

How inaccurate can people be and, also, how many innocent men have been vilified wrongly in the past! If there were individual observers I might be absolved on occasion from suspicion of having been participating in post-midnight, alcoholic orgies. It might ultimately be established that myself and men like me are not nearly as bad as we are painted. It might even emerge that I was preoccupied with the laudable task of conveying a drunkard to his doorstep instead of leaving him to his own foolish devices out of doors after dark.

The pooling of knowledge has always resulted in an improvement in man's perilous position on this wayward sphere whereas uncorroborated evidence has often resulted in grievous miscarriages of justice. I would therefore recommend that these after-dark peepers get together not just for my sake alone but for the sake of humanity as a whole.

25

However on a personal basis I would be deeply indebted to window-peepers everywhere were they to foregather at an early date and provide a comprehensive account of my witching-hour comings and goings if only for the fact that an accurate record be left for posterity.

A Stolen Pan

THE TIME 11.55pm. The year circa 1940. The place the back kitchen of a public house in Listowel. *Dramatis personae* four male poker players, one widow and a country cousin. It is the Lenten period and there is a mission on in town.

As we open we note the four poker players seated at a table near the fire. Each has a partly-filled pint glass of stout in front of him. The widow who is proprietress of the premises sits knitting at another side of the fire. There is a knock at the door. It is a familiar knock. The widow rises and admits a country cousin who brings her a gift of a satchel of freshly filled pig's puddings and porksteak fillets with the proviso that himself and the four poker players are to participate in the repast. The widow points out that the time is midnight and indeed as she speaks the clock in the bar clears its throat and confirms that it is indeed twelve o'clock.

'If we put them on now,' said she, 'we will be breaking the fast and we'll be committing a sin.'

The senior of the four poker players withdrew the family frying pan from under the table and announced that he had it on Papal authority that one could eat meat and meat products to wit pig's puddings until twenty-five past twelve. He was supported by the widow's cousin and by two of the poker players.

'Put them down now,' he instructed the widow, 'or they may not hold till Saturday.' No fridges in those days remember!

The widow greased the pan with dripping and laid the strips of pork thereon. She then cut the rings of freshly-filled puddings into inch-long cubes and waited for the pork to be turned. Ah what a sizzling and hissing there was when the puddings were added to the pork. A mouth-watering aroma assailed every nostril in the kitchen. Suddenly the poker player who had not voiced approval jumped to his feet and said that he would not have hand, act or part in the proceedings. So saying he opened the back door, looked up and down the backway to see if there were any civic guards concealed in the shadows and then vamoosed in the general direction of his home.

The senior of the poker players ordered four pints of stout for those who remained. Meanwhile the goods are frying happily in the pan. The widow busies herself in the bar while the four keep an eye on the frying pan.

When she returns with the four pints the puddings require turning. The aroma is intensified and one can hear the saliva slopping in the mouths of the watchers.

Finally the pan is lifted from the range and the senior of the poker players locates a loaf of bread and a pound of butter. Another provides plates and cutlery. Another rinses out the teapot while the country cousin rubs his hands in gleeful anticipation.

Before the widow has time to transfer the contents of the pan to the plates there is a knock at the door. It is the house-knock, known only to customers.

'Leave the hoor outside whoever he is,' advises the senior of the poker players.

'I can't do that,' says the widow. With pan in hand she goes to the door, opens it and looks out. All she can see in the dark is the outline of a man wearing a black coat and hat. Then her hand flies to her bosom when the round collar is revealed. Before the pan falls from her hand in shock the man with the white collar retrieves it. The widow staggers into the kitchen still clutching her bosom and gasping for breath.

'It's the missioner,' she whispers in terror. The poker players and the country cousin rush to the open door but there is nobody to be seen. Neither is there any sign of the frying pan or its contents.

How did the missioner know, they asked themselves? Had he just been passing and being subject to the same cravings as themselves was lured to the back door by the aroma? But how could he have known the secret knock? Divine inspiration maybe!

To this very day the mystery of the disappearing frying pan is still discussed. Unchristian souls insist it was the poker player who had earlier departed the kitchen. There wasn't an iota of proof against him, however. The moral here is that you should never allow a woman answer the door bearing a frying pan filled with puddings and pork.

Home-Town Decisions

IT MAY not read as such but this story is really all about the ignominy of home-town decisions. The home-town decision becomes inevitable when there isn't a clear cut difference between opposing factions. Some people would never be heard of but for home-town decisions.

Anyway I was the victim of one such decision as you shall see. I was the victim of some minor ones up to this so that you might say I should have been prepared but there are some experiences from which we never benefit and holding forth in foreign fields may well be one of the more significant.

Did you know that it was H.W. Longfellow who wrote the verse:

> *There was a little girl*
> *Who had a little curl*
> *Right in the middle of her forehead;*
> *And when she was good*
> *She was very, very good*
> *But when she was bad she was horrid.*

People may tell you that it wasn't written by Longfellow but you can take my word for it that Longfellow was the man, H.W. Longfellow, who died in 1882, at the age of seventy-five, who was a decent poet and a good man.

The reason I bring it up is because I was in a pub in a distant county a few short weeks ago. I was introduced to the daughter of the house, a charming six-year-old and quite a character to boot.

After a while she began to dance and in so doing knock-ed an innocent bystander's partly-filled pint glass to the floor where it broke and spread its contents on the carpet. The little girl covered her face with her hands and sat on a low stool nearby, fearfully contemplating her crime.

Like many a partly-spilled glass in public house history its owner claimed that it was more full than empty at the time of the spilling thus obliging the publican to re-place it with a full pint or at least three-quarters of a pint.

Isn't it the same with greyhounds? How speedier they become after being done to death by the passing transport. How shine their past accomplishments! How rosy their futures! How irreplaceable the loss!

I once killed a Rhode Island Red cock on my way to Tralee from Lyreacrompane. I called at once to the house from the gateway of which the cock had suddenly emerged. It transpired, according to the woman of the house, that there had never been such a cock. The hens would never be the same again. The woman who owned him would never be the same again. The very household would never be the same. I felt I was getting off lightly when she accepted a tenner.

But that's not what we're here to talk about. Forgive the digression. Recently I tend to wander away from the true flight of my narrative especially after weddings and other outings. I propose now to proceed unimpeded.

As soon as the glass was replaced by one which hosted a brimming pint a man with a lager in front of him pointed his finger at the little girl and quoted Longfellow's verse about the little girl.

'Amazing man Longfellow,' I said as I raised my glass. There was a respectful silence while I swallowed, not for what I had said but for what I was in the act of doing. It is churlish beyond words to interrupt a man while he quaffs the drink he has paid for.

'What has Longfellow to do with it?' asked the man

whose drink had been replaced as soon as he saw that I had completed the swallow.

'He wrote it,' I said calmly.

'He wrote it!' he echoed and then he laughed.

'He did not write it,' he said. 'I saw that in a book of nursery rhymes and they were all anonymous.'

'He wrote it all right,' I told him, 'and he also wrote "The Village Blacksmith" and "A Psalm of Life" and "The Song of Hiawatha".'

Having concluded I knew at once that I had committed the unforgivable crime of going on too long. We all do it at times.

'I know he wrote those,' he said truculently, 'so does every fool that walks the road but he didn't write "There was a little Girl".'

I decided to withdraw from the argument but it was not to be. 'I'll bet you a fiver,' said my tormentor, 'that it wasn't written by Longfellow.'

'All right,' I agreed against my better judgment, 'you're on.' I was on a good thing. I had no doubt. I wasn't going to crow about it. There had been enough of that.

We produced our fivers and handed them to the barman. I wondered how the bet would be settled. He must have heard me thinking.

'There's a man over there in the corner,' said he, 'that used teach English. In fact he learnt myself English.'

The man in the corner arose at my antagonist's behest and made his way to our part of the bar. He looked scholarly and perhaps his decision might be the cause of putting this lout in his place. He pondered for a goodly while before dispensing a decision. He took particular stock of my appearance and my dress which struck me as odd since they would not weigh in the balance.

'One thing is sure,' he said after a while, 'it wasn't wrote by Longfellow.'

'But it was,' I pleaded. He shook his head.

'You know everything don't you?' he said.

'I don't,' I assured him.

'Longfellow didn't write it,' he assured the barman. 'It's only an oul' children's rhyme and it's not the sort of lightweight stuff that a man like Longfellow would write.'

'Hand over the bet,' said the man who had laid it. The barman did as he was told.

There's an important moral here and it is that one must never trust a local referee and that way you won't be the victim of a home-town decision.

The winner smoothed out the notes and put them in his pocket. He didn't even ask me to have a drink as any decent human would.

If ever a man deserved to lose that fiver it was I. I asked for it the moment I announced that Longfellow was the author. I was setting myself up as an authority instead of minding my own business and keeping my knowledge to myself.

There is nothing as valuable as a shut mouth in a strange place. Opening it in foreign surroundings is akin to a stray dog barking for trouble when he is far from home. Haven't you all seen the cut of stray tomcats returning from forays into strange, moonlit territories? Scratched and bleeding they have paid the price for seductive meeowing in the principalities of other cats.

I daresay I was lucky to get off with the loss of a fiver. Like the tomcat or the stray dog I might have just as easily been assaulted for sounding off in another dominion.

Things are not too bad when one escapes so lightly in a world which is so well seasoned with the salt of injustice.

A New Englander

THE LAST time I was in New York a man came up to me in a bar and asked me if I wanted a bodyguard. I laughed, thinking he was joking.

'Who,' I asked, 'is going to mind you while you're minding me?'

He didn't see the joke. He assumed a fighting pose.

'Move off buddy,' said the elderly relative through marriage with whom I was drinking. Later that night we moved across the street to another pub where a serious argument was in progress. The holy name was taken several times as was the Holy Ghost's and God the Father Almighty's. The only conclusion that I could come to was that the fiery debate had to do with the nature of the three divine persons. I've heard stranger arguments in New York.

Soon arms were swinging, bodies jostling, cries ascending and what have you.

'It would be a wise move,' I said to my partner, 'if we were to remove ourselves before we get hurt.'

He was nowhere to be seen. I was disappointed but on the other hand how could I blame him. He was an elderly fellow, of nervous disposition and cautious outlook. When I emerged from the pub he was standing at the end of the block with his hands in his pockets. He seemed to be whistling. When I chided him for deserting me he laughed.

'A good bodyguard,' said he, 'always takes care of his own body first.'

'That's just another interpretation of the eleventh commandment,' I told him.

'Right first time,' he agreed, 'man mind thyself is what it says. It don't say nuttin' about man minding his in-

34

laws which is what you are.'

His comment surprised me. When I met him by appointment earlier he seemed a taciturn enough sort of fellow but after the intake of several shots of scotch and several steiners of Weisburger he had begun to tell me what good buddies we were and how buddies should stick together particularly buddies who were in-laws.

He had once been in Ireland with his wife who was a relation. They nearly ate us out of house and home. They also drank their fill at my expense but on the credit side they warned us that if ever we got to New York to be sure and look them up.

We looked them up but all they could offer was to meet us for a drink in a bar near the hotel where we were staying. He arrived on his own explaining that the wife could not make it because the dog was sick. After a while my wife excused herself on the grounds that she was tired. We dropped her at the hotel and returned to the bar. As I have explained we were forced to evacuate and take refuge in another bar.

After a few more scotches my in-law explained that he didn't like Catholics which was fine by me because there are quite a number of Catholics I don't like myself. At least we had something in common.

He then explained that he would have to leave as he and his wife and the dog would be going to Florida for the remainder of the winter, two days hence. In America, or at least New York, the custom when buying a drink is to leave your change on the counter until you are leaving. Then you leave a few dollars for the barkeeper and pocket the rest.

It occurred to me that I had seen none of my in-law's dollars on the counter. I pointed this out to him, well fortified by drink at this stage and mindful of the marvellous times he had promised us in New York while he was eating our food and swilling our whiskey back in Listowel, Ireland.

'Oh!' he said, 'I don't care if I drink or not. That's why I don't buy none. I can take it or leave it. I'm a New Englander you know. I never been drunk in my life. You wanna buy drink it's okay by me.'

A Hostile Corner Boy

SOME PEOPLE who have noted my many observations on corner boys sometimes ask me if the corner boys ever resent what I write about them.

'I mean,' a man said to me recently, 'you often mention that you can see them from your window. They know that they are the corner boys you're writing about. If it was me I wouldn't like it because I think what you write is provocative. In fact I think I would probably send you a solicitor's letter.'

I told him I was glad he brought the subject up as I am sure readers would be interested. The truth is that of all the corner boys described in these columns only one showed any signs of resentment. The others seem not to care and, in fact, one approached me recently of a Sunday morning and shook hands with me, complimenting me on my powers of sagacity and perception.

The mother of another told me that her son had given up being a corner boy after reading about himself. I was sorry to hear this because he was a dedicated corner boy and a great source of inspiration to me personally. He abandoned cornering altogether and found gainful employment in a local factory. He is now a part-time corner boy but the professional touch is missing.

Anyway enough of that; let us refer now to that solitary corner boy who resented my writing about him and his equals.

My first indication of his displeasure came one night in the middle of a pub quiz. My team were playing an away game and the venue was crowded. There I was with the rest of the onlookers vainly racking my brains for the answer to a difficult eight marker. The question had been 'What

great event took place in Clare on 24 June?' Nobody knew
the answer. The answer, of course, was the fair of Spancel
Hill. The clue lies in the lines:

It was on the twenty-third of June
The day before the fair.

Anyway upon lifting my pint with a view to swallowing
some of its contents I got a fairly solid thump on the back.
When I turned round I found myself confronted with an
extremely drunken and hostile face.
　'What's the idea?' I asked.
　'Think you're smart don't you?' said the man who had
delivered the thump. His eyes were bloodshot. His teeth
were bared and there was a snarl to him.
　A lesser man than myself might have quailed.
　'What's up?' I asked. Ordinarily I would ignore such a
thump but the fellow had made me spill the greater part of
my pint.
　Now the Keanes are normally a reasonable bunch although quick to anger when wronged. They'll not look for
trouble but they won't lie down either. You might kick a
Keane on the shin without fear of physical retaliation. You
may even stand on his corns or obscure his view but there is
one thing you must never do and that is spill his drink. The
Keanes are pernickety in this respect. When I pointed out to
the offender that he had indeed spilled my drink he
responded that he would just as soon spill my blood.
　'You're a great fellow writing about corner boys', he
said and again he ground his teeth. It was only then I remembered that I had indeed written about him. What I
had written was not in the least derogatory. It was the way
he interpreted it or worse he probably heard it second-
hand from a mischief-maker who distorted it.
　'Now my friend,' I informed him, 'let there be no more
thumping.'

'I am not your friend,' he stormed.

'Quiet please!' The injunction came from the quiz master. There the argument ended. As I said he was the only corner boy that I know of who resented my writing about him.

He still frequents corners and occasionally he looks up at my window as if he were daring me to come out and face him on his own terrain.

I will concede that he is a first-rate corner boy. He never obstructs passers-by. He never answers people who seek directions. He disappears at the first sign of trouble. He looks into space all day long and, generally speaking, does all that is required of a typical corner boy. Aspiring corner boys please note!

Beef Tea

I AM certain that there are many people who have never heard of beef tea much less drank it. When I was a gorsoon there was a famous greyhound in my native town who was once backed off the boards at Tralee track. He was well trained for the occasion and specially fed as the following couplet will show:

> *We gave him raw eggs and we gave him beef tea*
> *But last in the field he wound up in Tralee.*

Beef tea in those days was a national panacea as well as being famed for bringing out the best in athletes and racing dogs. Whenever it was diagnosed by the vigilant females of our household that one of us was suffering from growing pains we were copiously dosed with beef tea until the pains passed on. The only thing I remember in its favour was that it tasted better than senna or castor oil.

I remember once my mother enquiring of a neighbour how his wife was faring. Apparently the poor creature had been confined to bed for several weeks suffering from some unknown but malicious infirmity.

'Ah,' said the husband sadly, 'all she's able to take now is a drop of beef tea.'

She cannot have been too bad for I had frequently heard of invalids of whom it was said that they couldn't even keep down beef tea. When you couldn't even keep down beef tea it meant that you were bound for the inevitable sojourn in the bourne of no return.

Of course it was also a great boast for a woman to be able to say that all she was able to stomach was beef tea. It meant that she was deserving of every sympathy because it

40

was widely believed that if a patient did not respond to beef tea it was a waste of time spending good money on other restoratives. It was also a great excuse for lazy people who wished to avoid work. All they had to say was that they were on beef tea and they were excused. No employer would have it on his conscience that he imposed work on people believed to be on their last legs.

On another occasion as I was coming from school I saw a crowd gathered outside the door of a woman who had apparently fainted a few moments before.

'How is she?' I overheard one neighbour ask of another.

'They're trying her with beef tea now,' came the dejected response. The woman who had asked the question made the sign of the cross and wiped a tear from her eye.

There was another man in the street at the time, a notorious rogue albeit a likeable enough fellow. He was greatly addicted to all forms of intoxicating drink and as is the case with such people he frequently found himself with an insatiable desire for meat. He would insist, upon arriving home from the public house, that his wife did not look at all well. As it so happened she was something of a hypochondriac and liked to hear such things.

'I haven't been feeling well all day,' she would agree.

'What you need,' he would say, 'is a nice mug of beef tea. If you have a shilling or two handy I'll go down and knock up the butcher and get a pound of the finest round.'

All beef tea consisted of by the way was the water in which the beef was boiled. As soon as she started to partake of the tea our friend would start to partake of the beef. It was a good ruse and it kept both of them in good health for many a year.

Nowadays there is no talk of beef tea and more's the pity because I might not be here at all only for it. There were occasions when it was supposed to have brought people back from the very mouth of the grave. Under no circumstances was the fat of beef to be used. A nice lean cut off the round was the very man for the job.

People may look askance at it now but in my boyhood it was held in reserve to the very end much like a crack battalion in time of battle. Then when all seemed lost the beef tea like the battalion was successfully unleashed upon the enemy, the battalion upon the opposing army and the beef tea upon the harbingers of human extinction.

A Preview

HOW PROUD we would be if only we could see previews of our own funerals! What a shame that the deceased cannot acknowledge the regard of those who loved him not in life but lauded him in death. How oft have I heard the golden leaves of praise falling like benedictions when a departed soul was being transported to the graveyard.

'He'd give you the bite he'd be eating,' says the old man with the hat and the walking stick.

'He'd give you the shirt off his back,' from the old woman with the shawl.

'A great man to stand his round,' from the red-eyed man at the rear of the funeral.

'He had a heart like a mountain,' from a man with whom he had not exchanged a single word in forty years. The bother is that you put all of the aforementioned people on the rack and blistered their feet with cinders you would not get them to utter a solitary word of praise regarding the faithful departed when he was alive. There are many who spend long years preparing for their own funerals and there is nothing wrong with this but for the fact that a life is to be lived until the very last breath.

Instructions as to what should be worn by the deceased are frequently given by the deceased in the long run to expiry. I remember being a witness to a ferocious argument between an elderly brother and his sister not too long before they both drew the last of all their breaths. He had been out on the town the night before and he announced that it was his intention to go out on the town again that very night.

'You oul' fool,' said she, 'fitter for you be readying yourself for the hereafter.'

'I'll cross that bridge,' said he, 'when I come to it,' which brings us to the question uppermost in the minds of many old folk and that is how long should we spend preparing for that final journey or should we prepare at all — only plug away until our time arrives? It's a tricky question surely.

Let us return for some enlightenment to the argument which I heard between the old man and the old woman. When he returned after the second night's carousing she was very annoyed indeed.

'Have you your funeral money put to one side?' she asked. To him such a question did not merit an answer.

'Aren't you the cracked oul' man,' said she, 'going around like a gorsoon and you as old as the hills.'

'All I am is seventy-seven,' said he, 'and 'tis soon enough I'll be too old for diversion.' With that he sprayed the areas under both of his arms with deodorant and submitted his ears to a dart of same for good measure.

'Down on your knees you should be you scoundrel,' the old woman persisted with her harassment much to her brother's annoyance.

'I have only one life,' said he as he combed his wispish hair, 'and the Catechism don't say nothing about courting or carousing in the hereafter.'

At this the sister flew into paroxysms of righteous rage and declared that his soul was undoubtedly bound for hell where his flesh and limbs would get the roasting they deserved.

What her brother was really doing was protesting with all the means at his disposal against the prison of old age where the sister would confine him. The association of ideas which he would never accept were age and death. This is how old people are often seen, as nothing else but coffin fodder and small blame to them if they rail against it.

This treatise began with the notion that a man should

somehow be permitted to hear himself being praised at his own funeral. To achieve this all one has to do is go along to other funerals. Look long and listen well, all the time placing yourself in the position of the deceased. By doing this you will have a pretty good idea of what to expect at your own obsequies.

A Cuds and a Kishneen

AN ELDERLY friend of mine was once invited to stay with a lady who felt that he was in need of a holiday. She didn't ask him out of the blue. She had known him over a number of years, had seen him praying in the local church, had heard him answer the responses with great clarity at mass, had seen him on his rambles addressing himself to old and young with unfailing courtesy.

She came on holiday to the town at least once a year with a friend. They stayed at a high class guesthouse and at night they would frequent one of the several public houses of their choice. It was here that they heard my friend play the jew's-harp or, more correctly, the jaws' harp. He was the only person of their acquaintance who played the jew's-harp. He wasn't a very good player and it wasn't a very musical instrument so they were amused.

His *piece de résistance* was the 'Warsaw Concerto' although he rarely played it for the good reason that local blackguards would not give him a hearing. They did not physically restrain him but whenever he started they opened up with loud conversations and even encouraged other patrons to sing or dance. In short they were sick of the 'Warsaw Concerto.' It was different when the ladies were present. Out of respect for the pair there was silence when they requested the concerto. Even those who might otherwise offer a discouraging guffaw clapped deferentially at the conclusion.

Our friend would acknowledge the applause with a sweep of his right hand and graciously accept the half pint of stout which the ladies insisted he have.

Over the years the lady who eventually invited him on the holiday would arrive with different female companions. For her part she could not even contemplate her annual holiday any place else. Her car had once broken down in the town square and a passer-by, a native of the place, had come to her aid, re-started her car by rendering the choke ineffective and recommending to her and her companion of the time a cosy guesthouse in the town's immediate suburbs.

Here she was greeted effusively. Tea and sandwiches at no extra cost were pressed upon her. A bath was at once available and all this, mark you, at the height of the summer season. She was quite carried away as the saying goes. Breakfast consisted of porridge, fresh orange juice, several varieties of brown bread, all home made, scones, toast and the usual variations of bacon, egg, sausage, tomato, kipper and that all-too-absent ingredient of the breakfast table, the humble black pudding for which most visitors long but so few receive.

Who would blame the good lady if she fell immediately in love with the town? The public houses delighted her, particularly the one where our friend the jew's-harp exponent could be said to be the musician-in-residence. Years came and went and our visitor's hair began to turn grey but she was still a fine figure of a woman and still well entitled to the bracket known as the middle age. Shortly before her departure on her final holiday in the town she extended the invitation to the jew's-harp player. He accepted with alacrity. He was in receipt of a modest pension from a semi-state job and from the moment of the invitation onwards he saved most assiduously for the great occasion.

Eventually he boarded the train and was borne away to the great metropolis where he was greeted by our female friend and a number of companions who came to the station with her just for the crack as they say. An exhilarating time followed with visits to all of the city's best-loved night spots. Over the weekend there was a trip to the Wicklow hills and, all in all, the musician from our native town was accorded a reception fit for a king.

Alas, as all good times do, the holiday came to a close. On the morning of the penultimate day the good lady arrived at our friend's bedroom with a tray of breakfast things. He had expressed a liking for pig's liver some days before and two substantial slices of this nourishing and highly palatable pig produce graced his breakfast plate along with two outsize back rashers and I bet you have it guessed already, a sprig of watercress. I daresay his hostess was subconsciously paying back the town for all the kindnesses she had received there over the years.

Upon entering the room she found her friend, decently clad in slippers, pyjamas and dressing gown. He was standing by the window where he professed to be engaged with the watching of the blackbird colony in the shrubbery at the rear of the house. She placed the breakfast things on the bedside table and joined him at the window. Sure enough blackbirds of both sexes and every age were all over the place, their vocal appreciation of the morning's brightness not a whit unabated since dawn. The pair stood and watched.

'Your breakfast will be cold,' she said.

'There are more important things than breakfast,' said he.

'Oh!' was all his hostess said.

'What I would rather than any breakfast,' said he, 'is a cuds and and a kishneen.'

Puzzled, she searched her memory but could not recall the delicacy no matter how hard she tried. Her father had been a devotee of tripe and onions, her mother of boxty and a maiden aunt of colcannon but cuds and kishneen was outside her ken.

'I've never heard of it,' she said.

'I'll show you what a cuds and kishneen is,' he said and without another word he placed an arm about her waist and kissed her fiercely on the lips. She immediately broke from his grasp and fled from the room.

Disappointed he returned from window to bed but he managed to dispose of the entire breakfast nevertheless. He was surprised that she had never heard of a cuds and a kishneen which was simply a little cuddle and a little kiss.

His visit ended that day. She drove him to the station and bade him goodbye somewhat wistfully if not disappointedly. He could see that he had failed her, that their relationship would never be the same again.

Up until this time he had often confessed to himself that he had some difficulty in understanding the opposite sex. He would never understand them now. All he had done was to try and please her as he had done so many times in so many other ways.

I'm Only a Plasterer

ALWAYS TOWARDS the end of winter I savour past delights in front of my night-time coals. Aided by a pint of beer and a well-mustarded beef sandwich I summon up the occasions I enjoyed the most. How's that Shakespeare puts it?

> When to the sessions of sweet, silent thought
> I summon up remembrance of things past
> I sigh the lack of many a thing I sought
> And with old woes new wail my dear times'
> waste.

I rarely recall woes. I specialise in remembering moments of fun, lunacy and laughter. That is why upon this occasion I find myself obliged to journey back a few years to Listowel Writers' Week or rather that part of it when Irish Distillers so kindly sponsor the Irish coffee afternoon. There's many a steady man rolled home after that one.

Anyway there I was in the company of numerous, sonorous poets, doughty novelists and peering playwrights caught up in the considerable queue which had formed the moment it was announced that the Irish coffees were about to be served. There's a long story to be told about the prospect of free drink and the energy it induces in otherwise uncommitted people.

As I neared the entrance I was saluted by two friends of mine. Neither had any connection with the world of literature. One had once put down a floor for me and it remains as good as the day he put it down. The other was also a member of the building fraternity. I knew from their dispositions that they wished to gain access to the celebrations inside. Certain that the sponsors would have no objection I invited them in. Once inside we parted and circulated while countless glasses of excellent Irish coffee were consumed. The conversation slowly built up from a low hum to an animated buzz and then, as the liquor lifted all impediments from the flow of free speech, came the barking, the baying and the yelping and after that came the giggling and the gurgling and even guffawing as a happy time was being experienced by all.

Towards the close of the proceedings who should I meet but the man who put down the floor for me. He had a full glass in his hand and he stood listening politely to some ladies and a gentleman who happened to be holding forth about work in hand. Gratefully I accepted an invitation to join the company. I introduced my friend and after some more Irish coffees an extremely amiable situation existed all around.

We spoke of diverse matters relating to the writing trade and many helpful observations were submitted, considered and appreciated. Then one of the ladies addressed my friend. He had contributed his share to that most convivial of conversations but she felt that he had not declared himself sufficiently with regard to work in hand.

'Pray,' she asked most politely, 'what are you writing at the moment?' I was about to explain that my friend was a tiler and a plasterer and a blocklayer amongst other things but he was now replying himself.

'I'm only a plasterer,' he said.

'I'm only a plasterer,' the poetess repeated the words lovingly and reverently. The others took them up in quick succession, lost in admiration of what they believed to be a new and really original title.

'It's autobiographical of course,' the poetess was speaking again.

'I must get a copy when it comes out,' one of the gentlemen promised.

'It is probably the best title I have come across in years,' said another.

My friend and I decided to keep our own counsel. More Irish coffees appeared and from time to time one of the party would repeat the words 'I'm only a plasterer' and exclaim with longing that they would have loved to have conceived such an intriguing caption. Very often titles sell books and my good friend who was responsible for this one assures me that he will have no objection if some aspiring author would like to use it.

Sir

THE MAN I fear most in this world is he who calls me sir. If he is a gorsoon of tender years I do not mind for to be addressed as sir by such simply means that my middle age is being taken into account but to be addressed as sir by a man or woman older than me alerts me to the presence of deceit. Consequently I am wary thereafter and ready for anything so to speak.

Mock humility is the hallmark of a deceiver, submissiveness often the stepping stone to take-over and servility the breeding ground of arrogance.

The first man to call me sir was three times my age. I was immediately on my guard although my companions of the time insisted that the man in question was simply doing his duty.

I would have been eighteen when the incident happened. A party of us who had participated in a minor curtain raiser before an important senior football game in Tralee decided to venture down town for some refreshments before the big game commenced. We were assured by the man at the gate that we would not be charged anything on our return.

As I recall there were five of us in the company and when we returned there was a different man at the gate. When we tried to enter he stopped us and told us that we would have to pay. We explained that we had participated in the earlier game, that this was payment in itself and anyway that we had been assured of free re-entry by the man he had replaced.

'I'm sorry,' he said, 'but I have my orders and those are that nobody is to be left in without paying.'

He wasn't in the least bit arrogant. We asked him if

one of us might be allowed access in order to contact an official who would verify that our claim was authentic. He smiled rather sadly and turned away. I found myself growing annoyed.

'Look,' I said, 'at our boots and togs. Why would we have them unless we had been playing?'

'I'm sorry sir,' he said obsequiously, looking me between the eyes with the hideous obsequience of a fawning cur. 'I'm awful sorry sir but my hands are tied.'

What he was really saying was the following: 'I am in charge here and there is no way I'm going to admit impertinent scuts like you.'

He was a most respectable-looking man in his mid-fifties I would guess. In later years I saw him admit numerous cronies and toadies who simply shook his hand and passed him by without paying a penny. I once heard him described a true Gael.

On another occasion at a dance hall we asked the doorman to leave us in for half price as the dance was nearly over.

'I can't sir,' he said.

It was bad enough to be refused but to be addressed as sir on top of it was about as much as a body could bear. He was twice our age and was a shareholder in the hall. Also he had about a hundred acres of land and numerous other properties. It was rumoured too that he had his confirmation money. We had no choice but to pay the full admission price.

'Thank you sir,' he intoned his appreciation unctuously and when he thought our backs were turned a huge smile appeared on his face and he covered his mouth lest an outburst of laughter convey his true estimation of our rank.

Over the years I would meet many ingratiating wretches. Once I returned to a hardware shop to complain that I was a shilling short in my change. The clerk in question was the humblest of toadies, a known lickspittle without an ounce of character.

'I'm sorry sir, very sorry sir,' he spoke with obvious heartbreak and sincerity, 'but the rule is that you must check your change at the counter.'

I knew that he was laughing at me. We both knew that I hadn't a leg to stand on.

I don't mind waiters or waitresses calling me sir. That's their job. Americans too address others as sir in good faith but spare me from the fawning wretch who by calling me sir is really looking down on me, who knows he has more than I ever will and seizes every opportunity to avail of pseudo-servility in order to tell me so.

Thoughts for Christmas

CHRISTMAS IS the safety value of the human spirit and yet there are those who will not partake of it on the grounds that it is a load of sentimental mush. I meet them every Christmas and when wished a happy one they always respond favourably, give them their due.

There are still countries where Christmas has been officially abolished and there was a man in this very town of Listowel one time who used to go to bed for Christmas and re-appear when it was all over. I secretly believe that he was afraid of Christmas, afraid of what it might do to him. The same poor fellow lived and died a sourpuss leaving behind him vast sums of money, most of which his profligate next-of-kin spent on drink, horses and women and the remainder foolishly.

I love Christmas. It is my favourite festival and for weeks before there is a tingling in my being which suppresses the mean and the ignoble thought and which fondly reminds me of Christmas presents. The simple truth is that I could not endure the year without the bonus of Christmas.

Christmas to me is the wonder on a child's face, the quaffing of draughts and bumpers and the great unleashing of long-checked feelings which mantle the world with goodwill and love.

To those who have little time for Christmas I would suggest that they try a minimum dose of it. It has been known to work wonders for the disposition no matter how soured that disposition has been made by rejection or indifference. Christmas is the greatest of all the known antidotes for bitterness. It will cure instantly if taken properly and always with the most pleasant side-effects.

I say this with the full knowledge that Christmas is also a time of grief, a time for noting absences and a time for tears. Christmas without its instances of heartbreak is like an apple pie without cloves, a winter without thunder, a marriage without a row because if you give Christmas a chance you will find that it has the capacity to absorb heartbreak and to those of you who have the power to bring people together, whether sweethearts or those who have been sundered, spare no effort. Be infused with the spirit of Christmas and act now.

There is nobody so misguided as the man who believes he doesn't have the power to improve somebody's lot for Christmas. Goodwill is tangible. It never goes unnoticed. It can be felt by others.

One of the pleasantest Christmases I ever spent was celebrated in the back kitchen of our tavern. A crowd of us were seated around a turf fire in the back kitchen, the sanctum sanctorum where the spirit of Christmas resided throughout the 12 days and sometimes beyond.

There we were, happy as humans could be, as the hailstones beat frenetically on roof and window. Toasts went round and then Dick Roche spoke from his wheelchair.

'A happy Christmas,' said he, 'and thanks be to God we have our health.'

I remember too on that faraway Christmas how another man lifted his glass and made the most surprising toast of all. He was nicely sozzled at the time and afterwards could not recall what he had said.

'A happy Christmas,' said he, 'to the poor souls in hell' at which somebody proposed that hell be evacuated straightaway on the grounds that he had enough of it in his everyday life.

Dick Roche and his wheelchair are gone but how could I ever forget him? He liked to play a secondary role, to make light of his misfortune. I remember his eye was always filled with the gleam of concern for others and that is precisely what Christmas is all about and that is why Christ was born.

Christmas, by the way, doesn't come before its time. The year is about to expire and there is much to forgive and to be forgiven so that it's a good job Christmas comes the time it does.

I daresay the most priceless gift one could give in this day and age would be a drive home to a drunken reveller, precious because peoples' lives are involved. To really observe the spirit of Christmas in modern terms would be to maintain a vigil for potential drunken drivers, to deflect them graciously from their own steering wheels and not to fear rebuff or abuse in so doing. Now that would be a Christmas gift of the first water. Well might you toast yourself in the wake of such magnanimity.

Then, alas, there is the prospect that you will meet all too many fools who long for opportunities to deride Christmas and what it stands for. It takes all kinds they say.

Still when you meet a fool of this kind during the festive 12-day period treat him like a fool, that is to say with respect and courtesy, two benefactions for which fools always long but which they are seldom, if ever, accorded. In so doing you will diminish his disregard for Christmas and enhance your own.

Bores

IF YOU were ever waylaid by a neighbourhood bore, you would be well advised to seek sanctuary in the nearest church. Here the bore is not free to speak. He is forced to sit in silence.

Escape, therefore, into a place of worship is to be highly recommended and not only because it provides sanctuary from bores but also it should serve to remind us that we may have become remiss in the matter of daily prayer. Worshipful surrounds, more often than not, induce a holy line of thought. One can ponder too on one's lifestyle and resolve to make changes for the better.

The reason I write about bores on this occasion is that I feel I may have been too harsh the last occasion I dealt with them. From a personal point of view I am a victim of bores more than most and I have discovered that if you do not wish to give offence there is no really successful formula for evading them. It is bad manners when one brushes them off utterly. They must, therefore, be suffered to a limited degree.

In fact a minor bore can be of incalculable help in warding off the attentions of a major bore. In much the same way as commercial travellers bores have their own code the major feature of which is that one bore never intrudes when another bore is harassing a victim.

Your minor bore is the lesser of two evils but he can provide company on a dark night and he can keep a major bore at a distance. There is good in everyone even bores as I can truly testify and as readers will be able to deduce for themselves from the following story.

Many years ago I was engaged in a Gaelic football game in a distant village. It was during that era of the game's development when the accent was on the physical rather than the intellectual. Being a chap of high spirits I became involved towards close of play in a heated altercation which ultimately led to fisticuffs. Because my antagonist was a windy sort I coped with him easily. However, he warned me that his brothers would deal with me as soon as the final whistle was blown.

Sure enough as we left the pitch the brothers appeared with leaps and whoops not to mention a variety of threats that I was about to be destroyed and dismembered.

I braced myself for the onslaught. It never came, however, for no sooner had the game ended than a neighbourhood bore of the sporting variety came on to the field and collared me in order to convey certain reminiscences about his own doings on the field in his heyday.

Terrified lest I should dash off to the sideline and disappear in the crowd he placed a friendly but restraining hand upon my shoulder and proceeded to hold forth about a last minute point he had kicked in his twenty-first year while playing at centre forward with Listowel's second string against Ballybunion. The brothers who had earlier intimated that they were about to annihilate me stood undecided at a safe distance and pondered their new position. Revision was necessary because of the arrival of this doubtful newcomer.

At the very least, in their eyes, he had to be a relation, maybe a first cousin or even a brother. The fact that he had put his hand around my shoulder was ample proof that he was well disposed towards me. Now while the three brothers had no compunction whatever about taking on a single, slender townie, taking on two townies, one frail but the other large and fat was a different proposition altogether.

They hesitated for several minutes during which time they made numerous threatening gestures such as sticking out their tongues and pawing the ground with their feet.

Eventually, because the reduced odds were not to their liking they ran from the scene with high-pitched whoops and assorted threats.

Never before was I so grateful to a bore nor indeed was a bore so grateful to any listener for I remained on the field of play until I was absolutely certain that the brothers had departed for good.

During this time the bore reconstructed with uncanny detail the events which led up to the never-to-be-forgotten point scored so many years before.

He took account of the prevailing wind of the time, of its caprices and inconsistencies and the dispositions of the opposing backs as well as those of his fellow forwards. Remember that all of this took place in the three seconds or so between the time he won possession of the ball and the time he scored the point.

The moon was forfeiting its paleness to the approaching night as we walked off the pitch together. The price of survival had been high but it proved that bores have their uses. The moral here is that bores should be kept at bay for a rainy day and under no circumstances should they be permanently routed.

Capitol Pigs

IT IS a far cry from the Capitol of ancient Rome to the back sheds of these here licensed premises but the connection will duly manifest itself if the reader will bear with me for a while.

As I write the end of June draws nigh, sloppily and drearily and there is no hour that fervent aspirations don't assail my ear from farmers and shopkeepers alike who hope that fine days will appear and give us the semblance of a summer. Also as I write I see from my window two pigs standing in extreme befuddlement in the back of a trailer. Pigs are, by force of circumstances, creatures of habit used to regular feeding and regular hours. Hence the confusion on the faces of the pair beneath my window. If pigs were consolable by human words I could have reassured them and informed them that their hours had not yet come, that they were merely being transferred from one place to another where they would be fed and cosseted beyond their wildest dreams for several weeks until they were as fat as fools and fit for nought but slaughter.

Those two pigs transported me backwards in time, to the summer of 1956 in fact which was the year after I first acquired these licensed premises. I was then the proud possessor of two pigs of my own. I was talked into buying the pigs in question when they were mere bonhams by an uncle of mine who quite rightly suggested that they would eagerly dispose of any waste stout or slops thereby fattening themselves at no cost on the one hand and doing a professional disposal job on the other.

Let us now hasten back however to that memorable summer of 1956 which was a summer better than most. It was the year the late, lamented Princess Grace married

Prince Rainier. Who will ever forget the crass efforts by the English popular press to ridicule her and who will forget how abysmally they failed?

To make a long story short I made my way to the Listowel bonham market place with a friend well versed in the pig business and there we purchased a prime pair of bonhams for the modest sum of ten pounds. We were to receive no luck penny from the vendor as was the fashion but these bonhams would make their own luck in the course of time. They were cheerful bonhams but the same could not be said of their owner who, according to all his acquaintances, would not favour you with a solitary gumboil if he had a mouthful of same. He put the money in his pocket without a nod or a smile, cracked his reins dispassionately and guided his pony and rail through the dense traffic of the market place. We were obliged to take the bonhams home under our arms and after a period of initial squealing and squirming they settled down nicely after we departed the market place. On my way home I tried to recall where I had seen their former owner before. His face was as familiar as the sun or the moon or indeed any of the established landmarks of the countryside all around the town of Listowel and it was this that prompted my memory. I had seen his face before but not in town or country. Rather did I come across him in my many perusals of the family atlas, a venerable and well-thumbed tome which provided me with many a pleasant journey through various, far-flung corners of the world. The man who had sold me the bonhams was possessed of a head and neck the shape of Rathlin Island which stands aloof like a solitary inverted comma off the northern coast of Antrim. I have seen him on several occasions since and although I would frequently greet him with a wave of my hand he would never wave back.

The bonhams were duly installed in a small comfortable shed at the rear of the premises and there, as the summer days drifted by, they began to add on the flesh which would make them marketable later on in the year. They were as happy as the days were long. I allowed them out by day to root around the back yard, fed them with yellow meal and spuds, changed their bedding regularly and at night they were never without two or three pints of slops apiece which induced the most blissful and deep of slumbers. Their snoring was without snort or stutter. It was as soothing as the monotone of a summertime sea. Then one Sunday night the circus came to town and when it was over the streets of Listowel were thronged with thirsty circus goers who longed for a pint or two to dissolve the heady excitement of the slack wirewalkers and the bareback riders and the Mexican knife-thrower who had made the hair to stand upon their heads.

Being a publican I admitted a large number of these drink-deprived supporters of the arts although at the time it was against the law of the land. The beer flowed and the whiskey gurgled. The happy hum of conversation was everywhere as past acrobats and clowns long since departed were compared with the stars of the night's performance and then, suddenly, my wife informed me that our two pigs in the back shed were creating an almighty din. This was odd for they were normally the most tractable of chaps who never once woke from their stout-induced slumbers. As soon as a lull presented itself I made my way to the back yard at the end of which stood the shed which housed our two pigs. To say they were crazed would be to put it mildly. They sneezed and snorted. They ranted and raved. They tried in vain to break down the door of their sty. They ignored my protests and when I presented them with a bucket of stale porter they knocked over the bucket and spilled its contents.

Then I put myself a question. Are they trying to tell me something? Are they, I asked myself trying to warn me of impending doom like the geese of Rome's Capitol or

Killorglin's immortal puck goat? I silently climbed the roof of the backhouse and looked down. My heart stood still for below me were two members of the garda síochána one listening intently, the other standing close by. I knew it was only a matter of time before one of the pair would come to the front of the premises and begin the raid which would land me and my customers in court.

I slid from the rooftop without a word and rushed to the pub proper where I announced the presence of members of the garda síochána. All drinks were downed with a minimum of fuss and within one minute of my announcement the last of my customers had exited via the front door. Hardly had another minute elapsed when the limb of the law appeared. He was confronted by a deserted premises. He was delighted poor fellow for he had always maintained that his father would turn over in his grave if he ever found out that his son had raided a public house after a circus.

The pigs have long since gone. I sold them to a dealer rather than butcher them for my own use. I shall not look upon their likes again. Perhaps some poet will one day recall their services to mankind. They deserve to be remembered.

When things go 'bump' in the daytime

I THOUGHT, in my three score years in this vale of tears, that every aspect of public, human behaviour had been revealed to me. Oh vainglorious scribe that I am. I foolishly presumed that I knew it all regarding my fellow human beings!

I forgot that it is not within the scope of man to know all. Our brains are so puny and finite in comparison to the awesome revelations of the universe that it is not within our power to fully comprehend even the most obvious all of the time.

On my way to the hospital the other afternoon, to see a friend I was blithely tripping back Market Street when I encountered a human magnet. He came towards me at high speed, a stick under his arm, a cap on his head, wellingtons on his feet and a wild look in his eye. He was obviously on his way from the nearby cattle market. In many respects he reminded me of Young Lochinvar who came 'out of the west'. Remember:

Oh young Lochinvar is
come out of the west
And through all the wide
border his steed was the
     best.

He stayed not for brook and
he stopped not for stone.

And save his good broad-
sword he weapons had
none.

This man stayed for nothing either. He made weaving patterns as he moved, narrowly missing numerous other pedestrians. Then he bore down upon me.

Naturally, I moved to one side in order to avoid a collision but, dammit, didn't he also move to one side? It would have been fine if he had moved to the other side but no. He took it into his head to move to the same side.

Fortunately, we had both slowed sufficiently to avoid a serious head-on crash. We bumped against each other all right but no hurt was taken and no damage was done. The moment we touched we moved a step backwards. Then after a pause we decided to resume our separate journeys. It was not to be. The powerful inner magnetism that lies within certain people manifested itself to such a degree that every time I made a move he made one too.

The situation reminded me of a drover trying to stop an unruly heifer unused to highways and byways. The heifer will never go the way the drover wants her to go. He may flap his hands and call her every name under the sun but she will always do the opposite of what he wants.

It was the same way exactly with the farmer who confronted me and farmer he was without doubt. The only word he uttered was 'Currisht'.

Finally I decided that the only solution was to stop dead and to remain unmoving until he decided which way he wanted to go.

Alas and alack he did not know which way he wanted to go. The look in his eye suggested that I was deliberately trying to trick him into making a move that would be counteracted immediately.

He seemed to be mentally saying to himself. 'I have this knave of a townie figured out: I'll stop here till

67

doomsday, because I'm not going to let him make an ass out of me.' And so he stood while the world revolved all around. I stood as if in a trance.

Car horns hooted and the sound of brakes intruded from time to time. I could hear the cattle bawl in the nearby cattle market and a number of people who chanced to be passing by saluted me to no avail for I was lost in an unmoving pocket of time. It seemed as though I had been standing for an hour, whereas in reality it was only for about ten seconds but these are the sort of distortions that occur where one is trapped in such a fashion. To hell with it, I told myself, and gritting myself to the utmost or, as Shakespeare said, 'screwing my courage to the sticking point' I made a lightning move. So did he, and there we were — back in square one once more.

'I'll vault over you,' he shouted, 'if you don't clear the way.' And with that he prepared to vault.

Just then, however, a man I knew chanced to be passing by. He was a strong, hardy fellow, a relation of my wife's. Just as he drew abreast of us, I seized him by the belt of his overcoat and allowed myself to be dragged out of an otherwise, imponderable pucker.

The human magnet seized his opportunity and, with a whoop and a flourish of his stick, passed me by. The whoop might suggest that he had liquor taken but, from what I knew of him, I deduced that he was not a liquor man. He was a bun-eater, a type of countryman who gets rarer and rarer with the passing of every fair. He was also a human magnet. We all have the potential to be human magnets but most of us never mature beyond the occasional, ephemeral polarisation. The proper thing to do when you encounter a human magnet is to turn on your heel and vamoose in the opposite direction.

There is no point in trying to pass by. There is a long ritual to be gone through before safe passage is possible. I have never seen but I have heard of fist fights which have occurred out of magnetic confrontations. In fact I was once told of a certain gentleman long deceased who, when a student in the city, went around at night seeking human magnets.

Upon locating those unlucky enough not to move quickly in the opposite direction he would make straight for them like a battle cruiser, flooring them without mercy. When he had money he spent his time in one or other of the city's most hospitable hostelries but, because he was only a poor student, this was very rare indeed.

Eventually and inevitably, he met a larger lout than himself who floored him with a knee in the pelvis. The Marquis of Queensbury, then as now, had few devotees on the streets of the capitol and the most devastating of all blows in the common street confrontation was the Ringsend Uppercut. This was simply a kick between the legs.

Let us move away, however, from such unsporting pursuits and look at another aspect of human magnetism. The kitchen in the common or garden home is a great place for confrontations and, for many years, my wife and I would bump into each other with disastrous consequences. There I would be coming in the back door with a sack of turf and there would she be, going out with a bucket of water. In our younger days we were always in a hurry and, consequently, I was often caught napping.

My wife, a lady in all respects, drew the line at doorways. She simply kept going so that whoever was on the way in or the way out had to get out of the way. In my anxiety to grant her safe passage I underwent several heavy spills, the marks of which still remain after all the years. Love, however, inflicts no real pain and I cherish these blemishes as a veteran might cherish the marks of battle campaigns.

There are some people in public who are not designed or programmed to get out of the way of other people. This is because there are no laws governing the behaviour of pedestrians. At sea there is a law which insists that steam must give way to sail but there is no such law for pedestrians. Indeed, steam has the right of way in our streets and the slenderer, more graceful, females who resemble sailing ships often fall foul of puffing thugs.

A New Alphabet

I HAVE long believed that the letters of the alphabet are not placed in their proper or natural order. I will concede that you could not have a better or more placatory opening. The letters A, B and C strike me as an acceptable introduction for what is to follow.

The trouble begins when we come to the letters F and G. F, in my opinion, should not be permitted to precede G. It is linguistically inappropriate and it is artistically unapt as well as being phonetically false. I make no real complaint about the placings of the remaining letters although, on a purely personal and whimsical basis, I would have K before J.

JK sounds like a person's initials and gives an unfair advantage to people who are possessed of initials. I was a JK one time but I decided to stick a B in between in case people might think I was taking advantage of those who weren't as fortunate as I from an alphabetic point of view. Fortunately, B stands for Brendan and since Brendan is the patron saint of my native county Kerry I was adequately rewarded for any sacrifice I might have made. In the last analysis, however, virtue is its own reward.

Not only should G come before F but it is my considered opinion that it should be much nearer the beginning of the alphabet. G, you might say, is much the same as C in appearance and does not sound all that different so I would suggest that it might come after C.

I'm sure E wouldn't mind all that much. It has had a good innings and I don't think it is as colourful a letter as G. G is a fulsome letter with loads of body and appendages like no other letter in the alphabet. G, although it looks formidable, is anything but. It lacks the naked savagery of H and the dangerous buzz of Z, the alphabet's anchor man.

Let me make one thing clear before we go any further; I have nothing against any particular letter in the alphabet. If I like certain letters more than others you can put it down to taste. There is no ill-will, no animosity. I wish every letter well and would be the first into the arena in defence of any particular one.

For instance if Z were to be ostracised tomorrow I would organise a petition to have it restored to its rightful place. Vowels and consonants are equals in my book. I will doff my hat as respectfully to W as I would to E.

Seriously, however, I think it is high time that the alphabet got a right good shaking up. There have been too many letters in the same place for far too long. To show how broadminded I am I would not object if the whole contraption was turned around and had Z for front runner instead of A. In fact, you could start in the middle and go backwards and forwards if you so wished.

I really think that the fairest thing to do under the circumstances would be to put all the letters into a hat and have an open draw. First out would take pride of place and second out and so on.

I would suggest that this draw should take place every seven years or so but I would not mind if a year was given or taken. Let a commission appointed by the government decide upon such matters.

The important thing is to face up to the fact that the alphabet like everything else needs to be shaken up every so often. A stagnant alphabet could lead to stagnant literature.

A freshly re-arranged alphabet would lead to all sorts of changes and a change, as the man said, is as good as a rest.

How is that the poet Tennyson puts it?

The old order changeth yielding place to new
And God fulfils Himself in many ways
Lest one good custom should corrupt the world.

As the alphabet stands it is in no way demoralising nor could it be described as an evil influence. All I'm saying is that the time has come for change. All I ask is that the letters be re-shuffled. The government does it so why not the alphabet!

We grew up with the ABC. We've had it all our lives. How nice it would be if our children and our children's children grew up with the VIP or the PHD.

Human Gooseberries

I NOW propose to address myself to human gooseberries for the good reason that I have never done so before and neither, to my knowledge, has anybody else.

Edible gooseberries, as we all know, belong to the saxifrage family and to the same genus as the currant of which there are countless varieties. The gooseberries I have in mind belong to the human family.

Edible gooseberries are used to make tarts and jams and desserts whereas the human gooseberries are used to make longterm alliances between consenting males and females. Edible gooseberries are covered all over with bristles whereas the human gooseberry is only partially covered. The human gooseberry is full of bones whereas the edible gooseberry has no bones whatsoever. However the most important difference of all between the two is that the edible has no heart and the human has.

I was once a gooseberry. I was forced into the role by a female relative whose daughter was invited to a dance in Ballybunion by a local gentleman of considerable means but questionable reputation. The man in question was several years older than both the girl and myself. I was obliged to go along with the pair to make sure that they behaved themselves or rather that he should behave himself for in those days it was foolishly presumed that all false moves during such romantic skirmishes were made by the male of the relationship and that the female played a passive role.

Nothing in fact could have been further from the truth. When a female makes a false move, if you will forgive the expression, it does not necessarily have to be a physical one nor indeed a perceptible one, perceptible to none, that is, but to whom she wishes to perceive. The truth is that the simple arching of an eyebrow or the most insignificant flutter from the eyelashes can wreak havoc or create delight in the bosom of the male who happens to be the man in question at a particular point in time.

Far more intimidating and more impressive than any physical gesture she might contribute to a night's romantic proceedings would be, for instance, what unimaginative poets refer to as the flicker of a smile. This can uplift the spirit of a depressed partner as forcibly as a kiss for instance whereas a common or garden blush after a commonplace compliment can prompt the most reluctant of males into making a proposal of marriage. A female's real power is not in her hands or feet but rather in her repertoire of shy glances and winsome smiles.

To return, however, to my role as a gooseberry I recall that I, the gooseberry, and my charges entered a public house in Ballybunion where the man I had been detailed to watch endeavoured to make me drunk by trying to force large whiskies upon me at an unprecedented rate.

I must say, however, that my heart was not in my work and anyway the cousin's daughter was well able to look out for herself. I also felt that I was not born to be an onlooker in such a sport. Rather was I born to participate. In the ballroom our friend, after casting his eye about him, allowed the same orb to settle on an attractive girl of my own age. Introducing me he informed her that he was doing so at my express instigation, that I was a shy sort and had admired her from afar for many a day.

Flattery does not always impress the female of the species but it is far better than doing nothing at all. Soon we were dancing and later she was to entrust me with her purse. After I had escorted her to the car which would take her home I remembered my primary obligation. After a long search I discovered his car. He had parked it just above the strand which afforded a view of the shimmering night-time sea. They were in the throes of fervent courtship.

That was my first and last time playing gooseberry. The couple to whom I had been assigned eventually married and had several offspring so that it might truthfully be said that my gooseberrying had contributed in no small way to the propagation of the human species.

Female Corpses

I LISTENED enthralled the other night while a group of women recalled the most handsome and best laid-out corpses they had ever seen. They were, if you'll forgive the perishing pun, deadly serious.

One with a gin and tonic remembered the greatest corpse dresser of all time. She was known as Nell the Dead and when she prepared a female corpse for wake-room inspection the deceased always looked infinitely more beautiful than she had in life. In fact a drunken agricultural labourer who arrived late at the wake-house was so moved by the beauty of the corpse that he proposed to her there and then and what harm but he wouldn't give the creature a second glance in real life. Another gentleman, admittedly a notorious drunkard, is alleged to have absconded with the cadaver so taken was he by the beauty of her appearance and her refusal to reject his advances. Luckily he was stopped at the door of the wake-room.

No great notice was taken when an unfortunate member of the opposite species passed away. I'll grant you he received a rough and ready shave from the corpse dresser and his hair might have been racked as the saying goes but there was little beyond that save the re-adjustment of his false teeth, the crossing of his hands and the closing of his eyes. You'd never hear it said of a man that he was a handsome corpse. His friends might say 'God be good to the poor oul' hoor' but apart from the sorrow of his wife and family there would be no word regarding his appearance.

In my youth the majority of female cadavers were dressed in the Children of Mary costumes with the white veil sometimes covering, sometimes parted over the face. Now that's all changed and women dress more fashionably on predeceased instructions. Many choose a favourite costume with matching shoes while with others it might be a dress or a chaste brown habit. Long ago they were dressed for eternal repose. Now they seem to be dressed for nothing but travel.

I personally knew an oldish gentleman who never seemed to be able to get on with his wife. For her part she was a non-stop nagger and between the pair of them they managed to successfully smother the prospect of any happiness that was likely to surface during their better moments. She died before he did. He was ushered out of the way when the corpse dresser arrived. She was an extremely talented woman. Someone once said of her that she could transform a devil into an angel on the death bed. I have heard of other occasions where the surviving male was seen to wring his hands in frustration for not having fully availed of the beautiful creature during her life. Another became suddenly suffused with blushes and was too shy for a while to look at her. Anyway she set to work on the deceased and when the job was done the husband was summoned to see if he approved of the finished product. He was shocked beyond words when he beheld the gorgeous creature on the bed. 'Blasht her,' he said, 'why didn't she look like that when she was alive?'

Bitterly he turned to the corpse dresser and shook her by the shoulders: 'Goddamn you why didn't you do her up before this?' he asked bitterly.

It is rather odd, of course, that so many females should leave instructions that they should be fully made up for exhibition in the wake room but never having bothered much about their lifetime appearance as far as the unfortunate husband was concerned.

There was a particular case of a corpse which looked so beautiful that one man was obliged to leave the wake-room because he was experiencing impure thoughts.

A woman-hater of my acquaintance once explained to

me that certain women saw to it that they were absolutely beautiful in death in order to get their own back on husbands who had neglected them during life.

Often alas, the make-up was overdone and instead of looking the angel she had intended to be the unfortunate corpse looked more like a trollop.

A woman once told me that many left instructions that they were to be dressed to kill and made up like film stars in order to show their delight at parting from unkind mates. True or false one thing is certain and that is: no woman will miss a chance of showing off when she looks her best.

It is a subject which should not be treated lightly. That is why I am personally of the belief that there should be a competition for the best looking corpse in a particular community.

A Spoiled Corner Boy

I PROMISE that this will be my last contribution on corners and corner boys although strictly speaking I do not propose to write about corner boys at all on this occasion.

The chap I propose to present for your edification is no more a corner boy than my sainted grandmother and yet he leans more in the vicinity of corners than any corner boy. You have seen this rare specimen and it is likely that you have ignored him and taken him for what he is not, a corner boy. I too was taken in the first time I saw him. He comes to the corner, looks for a moment as if he is going to lean against it like any common or garden corner boy but then seems to suddenly change his mind.

He is, in point of fact, a countryman, a son of the soil, a milker of cows and castrater of calves. He is his own man and he is not as he has been so often mis-labelled a peasant or a churl or a bog trotter. He is neither a yokel or hick. He is a husbandman with time on his hands. I know for I too was called a hick by clodhoppers who forsook the country for the metropolis which is fine in itself if they remembered they were countryfolk before they assumed artistic pretensions.

We have therefore a middling-sized, hard-working, moderately well-off farmer who has momentarily forfeited his independence because he took a lift to town and left his own car at home. He is like a fish out of water at first but then, like the astute evaluation merchant that he is, he avails of the corner's unique vantage points to take in as much as is humanly possible in as short a time as possible.

From the corner he can see hither and over as well as up

and down. He misses nothing. He makes a mental note of every item in every shopping bag and when his wife will ask later that night in bed if he saw anything of interest in the town he will be able to regale her with a comprehensive account of the numerous happenings and sights to which he was a witness albeit for ever so short a time.

He could never aspire to the high vocation of fulltime corner boy. He would have seen all that was to be seen in a matter of minutes and unless there were cataclysmic happenings on a regular basis his patience would run out and he would run off.

If someone approaches him looking for directions to the bank or the post office he will not make the time-honoured reply 'I'm a stranger here myself'.

Rather will he enjoy the discomfiture of the man who does not know where the bank or the post office is and he will allow his belief that countrymen are infinitely better than townsmen to be reinforced. If he came to town to do business with a bank he would know beforehand where the bank was. You wouldn't catch him asking a stranger where it was. He is amused by the fact that a well-dressed, obviously well-heeled visitor feels the necessity to question a man who only knows enough to provide for himself. If it were himself he would have asked a man who looked like a townie. Only a fool would ask a visiting farmer for directions in a town.

During his few minutes vigil he notes the resident corner boy who languishes drowsily, for it is a warm day, with his back to the wall of the house which composes the corner. He would be prepared to exchange notes with him if his eye was catchable but catchable it is not.

People pass. Cars honk. Dogs differ. Women chat. Engines rev. Idlers dawdle. Commercials hurry. Vans deliver. Exhausts fume. Heels clip. Starters stutter and the business of the town is fully under way, each contributor playing its part.

Our friend's patience has run out. There's work to be done. Next time he would bring his own car and be dependant on no one. Feeling conspicuous and self-conscious now he looks at his watch and wonders what in blazes is keeping the colleague who gave him the lift. A minute late already, two, three. At last he arrives.

In the car there is silence for awhile, both occupants endeavouring to frame an observation to suit the occasion.

'Cripes almighty,' says our friend, 'the town is a quare place.'

'The town,' says his companion, 'is for townies.'

Happily they journey homewards, glad of their vocations. A town is a useful place but not for living in.

Lurchers

EVERY WEEK I meet a new kind of person. So what! the
cynic will say. No two persons are alike in the first place.
That's not what I mean. For instance I thought until
recently that I had encountered every type of drunkard
from the besotted to the articulate, from gentle to violent,
from the boring to the bullying and so forth and so on across
the great variety of topers, tipplers and alcoholic what-
have-yous.

There is no end, however, to the flow of hitherto un-
heard, hitherto unseen, hitherto unsmelt drunkards. All
you have to do is to keep your eyes open and if you are
sufficiently interested in the human condition you will be
richly rewarded.

I often laugh quietly to myself when I hear people say
that all the great characters are gone from the world. The
characters are still there waiting to be discovered but the
tragedy is that people have now less time and little inclin-
ation to go looking for them. Characters will never be in
short supply but astute observers allow their energies and
potentials to be consumed by television, to mention but one
of the many distractions of the age we live in.

Lately I heard a friend say that drunken men were
becoming scarcer and scarcer and that you'd never see a
really disgusting drunk these days.

I came across a new type of drunkard at the weekend,
new to me that is because I am certain that there are readers who have long ago encountered his ilk. I was emerging
at the time from a delicatessen where I had purchased
some coleslaw and cow's tongue.

The wife was away for the day so I undertook the

feeding of myself. Coleslaw, cow's tongue and bottled stout may seem a harsh diet to some but I always find it ideal fodder because as well as being nutritious it is exciting. Without excitement food is a mere filler. It becomes a force of habit rather than a taste bud tantaliser.

Coleslaw and tongue in hand, the latter pickled of course, I took to the street and headed for home. I have always maintained that surprise is the most potent element in any form of attack. A sudden, unexpected onslaught on even the most redoubtable of opponents induces such a state of initial shock that the victim is reduced to temporary helplessness. This is precisely what happened to me.

There I was, one minute journeying happily homeward to a richly-deserved repast and the next stunned and staggering, my coleslaw scattered to the four winds, my tongue plastered to the sodden street. For several moments while I tried to recover my bearings I presumed that I had been the victim of a deliberate assault from some individual who had suddenly become incensed by some unpleasant aspect of my physiognomy or some hostile wretch who may have at some time taken offence from one of my many public and sometimes disconcerting observations on matters topical and general.

As soon as the initial shock had spent itself I found that I had been struck head-on by a large, obese man in his cups. This, however, was no staggering stumbler. This was a lurcher, i.e., a drunkard who maintains a fairly straight course but who now and then lurches forward unexpectedly often unfortunately colliding with innocent victims who are completely unaware of his capacity for lurching.

Shortly after being struck I was tempted to haul out and lay a fist on the jaw of my assailant. Reason prevailed, however, and I kept my head, glad that I did for the collision was completely accidental. Your lurcher, although he knocks women and children to the ground, is never aware of the damage he causes. He proceeds happily if drunkenly on his way oblivious to the disasters in his wake.

Although fully aware, after several minutes, that I had been obstructed and almost felled by a lurcher I was still tempted to draw a clout or, at the very least, to wait until he had passed by when I might discreetly deliver a well-placed kick on the fellow's posterior. However, I have an old maxim and it is that one should never strike a drunken man or even argue with a drunken man. A body would be more profitably employed arguing with a bumble bee or trying to verbally dissuade an enraged bull from charging an innocent victim. In fact I would go so far as to say that it is sinful to strike a drunken man on the grounds that he cannot retaliate or defend himself.

It is perfectly correct, in my estimation, for one drunken man to attempt to strike another drunken man. Notice I say attempt to strike. You see gentle reader your common or garden drunken man is incapable of delivering a telling blow so it is perfectly all right if he attempts to do so.

Anyway it is a known fact that truly drunken men never come to any harm so when they fight the only danger is to the innocent passer-by who, because of poor eyesight or some other infirmity, might well find himself at the receiving end of a drunken fist.

Odd you might think that I had never come across a lurcher before but not so odd when you consider that he is not all that easily identified. For most of the time he walks in a normal fashion, fitting neatly into the flow of pedestrians so common to all busy thoroughfares.

The average onlooker must not be blamed if he presumes at first sight that the lurcher is sober and predictable. The fellow will keep pace with his fellow pedestrians until there comes a sudden eruption which follows a lurching pattern highly dangerous to innocent passers-by, particularly those burdened with groceries or with coleslaw and pickled cow's tongue as happened to me.

The only guard against lurchers is eternal vigilance.

We must, if we are to transport our goods to the safety of our homes, always be on our guard and we must conclude that every oncoming pedestrian may well be possessed of a drunken lurch.

When we take other pedestrians for granted we are submitting ourselves to the possibility of a disabling collision. Watch out, therefore, for that first, high, telltale step. It is the prelude to the lurch which might render you senseless, which may well scatter your coleslaw to the four winds and render your cow's tongue inedible.

The question arises as to how then anything can be done to save the limbs and peace of mind of the unwary in the face of the unexpected lurcher? I have given the matter a good deal of thought since my own encounter and I have come to the conclusion that it is not the lurcher who is to blame but his handlers, i.e., members of his family, his friends, his neighbourhood publican who are aware of his proclivity towards lurching and who are quite content to stand back and do nothing whatsoever about it.

There are many corrections which they might make. For instance, a harness might be devised which would be placed around the chest and shoulders of the lurcher. Attached to the harness would be a reins, should the lurcher embark upon one of his boozes he might be accompanied by a guide, say a neighbour or an unemployed member of his family. Then when he had imbibed enough liquor to render him drunk the guide might seize the reins and direct the poor fellow in a homewards direction.

As soon as the lurcher gives the slightest indication that he might be about to lurch the guide should immediately dig in his heels and come to a sudden halt, thereby restraining the lurcher from moving forcefully forward and flattening some luckless, oncoming pedestrian.

I'll grant that there are sensitive families who might not wish to see their own particular lurcher in harness. This is perfectly understandable but it does not relieve the family of responsibility for the lurcher's behaviour in public.

I, therefore, suggest some form of distinctive headgear which might be firmly rammed on the lurcher's head when alcohol has gotten the better of him.

A friend to whom I confided after my own first encounter with a lurcher suggested a type of placard upon which would be written the words: 'Caution. I am a Lurcher!'

In case the gentle reader thinks that I may be carrying things a bit too far let me remind him that lurcher victims often carry the mental and physical scars far into life apart altogether from the financial loss which can include the wreckage of groceries and breakage of bottles.

It is long past the time for castigatory tut-tutting and head-shaking. Action is called for before the victims start to retaliate.

A Genuine Tip

I NOW submit a strange but authentic tale. I suppose, in a sense, it could be called a case of mistaken identity. Judge for yourself, however. Draw your own conclusion. Maybe you've had a similar experience yourself.

Some time ago I paid a visit to Killarney Races. I didn't back a single winner but I enjoyed the racing, the incomparable setting and the glamour of the many delightful females present for the occasion. It was worth the visit for the shapes, colours, and sizes of the many interesting hats on view, not to mention the costumes, the shoes, the handbags and what have you!

I was given several tips but not one obliged. I wasn't disappointed because I don't really go to races to win. I go to enjoy myself and, perhaps too, to find material for my books and newspaper columns and so it was on that lovely May evening with the glitter of lakes and the serenity of soaring mountains in the background that I found the makings of a readable story. I stored it away for a while to let it mature. In this respect certain stories like certain wines improve with age.

With an old friend I partook of several bottles of nourishing beer and, believe it or not, two cream buns apiece which we purchased in the nearby dining area. I have an unbridled yearning for buns and often in city streets when I behold a pastry shop I am drawn indoors like a moth to a light bulb. We savoured our buns and beer in a quiet corner of the stand.

In between we would back our fancies and watch the racing until there came a time when the intake of beer compelled us to forsake the camaraderie of the bar for the gents' toilets.

'Always,' my friend advised, 'it is wise to keep your ears alerted in racecourse toilets for very often a lot more than buttons are slipped by the piddling punters. I have overheard vital pieces of information from time to time and, as a result, have backed many winners I might not otherwise have backed.'

Sure enough as we performed our duties we heard above the gentle cascading of numerous waters the following words of advice given by an elderly chap dressed in tweeds to a younger chap with a thin face and a jockey's slender frame.

'Never mind what her form's been like up to this,' the older of the pair was saying, 'put it all behind you and concentrate on the present time. Put the past firmly behind you and you could be on a red hot favourite instead of a rank outsider.'

'Yes, yes,' the younger man responded eagerly as they tied their fly buttons and headed for the exit.

Motioning me to silence my friend followed the pair out into the evening sunlight. They were still talking when I arrived.

The older man's face was now possessed by a most solemn expression as he looked the younger in the eye. That worthy, to give him his due, was the epitome of attention.

'Don't give her as much as a single stroke,' the older man was counselling, 'or you could unsettle her and all your efforts will be for nothing. There's some will take it alright and be the better for it but this one is bred otherwise so let you handle her with kid gloves.'

'No whip then!' the younger man said with a touch of a wry smile around his pinched mouth.

'No whip,' said the older emphatically, 'she'll go a damned sight better without it.'

Again the younger man responded agreeably. He had a jockey's athletic body, the finely chiselled features, the aquiline nose, in short, all the attributes of the professional horseman. I was about to depart in the direction of the parade ring when my pal forestalled me.

'Not yet,' said he, 'not yet.'

I indulged him and waited a while longer but nothing more seemed to be forthcoming. Then suddenly the old man placed a fatherly hand on the younger man's shoulder.

'Don't mind what you're told about her,' he counselled, 'she'll take any fence with you if you don't push her too hard.'

'What's the final word then?' the younger man asked before heading towards the jockeys' room to don his silks.

'The final word!' the older man echoed as he pondered deeply and scratched his chin.

'My final word,' said he, 'is to take her easy in the early stages, hold her up so to speak and then when she gets used to you and used to the course you can start nudging her. Give her a few pats when you come to the straight and you'll make that winning post no bother.'

The pair shook hands, the younger man going his way and the older presumably to the owners' and trainers' enclosure.

My friend, ever an enterprising fellow, followed the older man and waylaid him with the following words: 'Would you tell us her name like a decent man. Neither my friend nor myself has a single winner backed this night.'

The old man looked at him and a puzzled look appeared on his kindly face.

'Whose name?' he asked.

'The name of the mare you were talking to your jockey about.'

The old man threw back his head and laughed loud and long.

'Ah God help you,' said he, 'she's not a mare at all and he's no jockey. He's a neighbour of mine that's after getting married this morning and he just asked me for a few words of advice.'

'Oh,' I said apologetically, 'forgive us.'

'Think nothing of it,' said the old man. 'I'm a veteran of over forty-five years in the marriage stakes so you could say that I know the ropes.'

'I should say so,' I agreed.

'You see,' he said, 'this lady he married hasn't had such good form up to this and what I really tried to get across to him was that the past is past and it's the future performance that matters in all marriages.'

On our way back to the train my friend laid a hand on my arm. There was a smile on his face.

'I was right,' he said.

'In what way?' I asked.

'Well,' said he, 'we went into that toilet looking for a tip and we got a genuine one!'

The Definitive Diagnoses of Balthazar B.

REMEMBER THAT I am a man who used to advertise butter on television. I did it for a number of reasons. One was as good a reason any man could have for doing anything. I got paid for it.

I also did it because I genuinely liked butter and could not live without it. I used to smear it on everything from toast to potatoes to biscuits to cheese.

I couldn't knock any satisfaction out of cheddar cheese unless I smeared it with butter. During the war years I pined for butter. It was rationed. We only got two ounces per head every week.

While I was off the butter I found no peace. I tried replacements and they were all right. I daresay they were adequate but I had an insatiable craving for butter although a doctor Hoodleflier from Pennsylvania said it was bad for the heart.

I went back on the butter and forgot Doctor Hoodleflier. There's no week since that I don't read articles about the goodness and badness of butter. The truth is that if butter agrees with you, you should eat it and to hell with what half-potted experts say.

The only true expert about food is your friend Doctor Balthazar Belly whose address is Mid-Body Mews, Interior Area, Human Anatomy, in other words your own tummy.

Some years ago I wrote a fairly lengthy treatise in which I suggested that there should be some sort of machine which would record our belches and deduce from the strength and quality of the belch the nature of the problem in the tummy.

Now, I propose to go a step further. There should be a foundation which would finance a system whereby each and every one of us might have access to the opinions of Doctor Balthazar Belly of Mid-Body Mews.

Believe me when I say that nobody knows more about our health than our beloved Belly. When he protests look out. When he gurgles or snarls it means that there is something wrong.

There are times when he may gurgle happily like a baby but there are other times when the gurgles can be as ominous as the first splutterings of an erupting volcano.

When we would lift our phones to dial our own bellies the results might not be immediately understood. I suggest that there should be a scrambler built into each phone unit.

For instance if I am assailed by a sudden pain in the chest I should, of course, ring my doctor at once.

However, while I am waiting for my doctor I might put the call through to the belly whose gurgling and rumblings would be magnified. When these are fed to the scrambler we would be in receipt of curt messages such as:

'Why did you have to eat that extra sausage you accursed glutton?' or 'you have my heart broken so you have in my endeavours to digest the fat meat which you persist in feeding me' or 'you have me drowned entirely from the waves of beer you send washing all over me' or 'you have me scalded altogether with whiskey you drunken wretch.'

Nobody knows better than Doctor Belly himself. The system would not be costly for the simple reason that it would be a requirement for everybody. It would also be of invaluable assistance to doctors in the short term who might immediately assuage pangs of pain after a brief study of Doctor Belly's revelations.

In the long term the system would be of incalculable value. We would know what foods to avoid and how much drink to drink, down to the nearest minim.

Any man with access to his own tummy is already halfway towards a healthy life and then, of course, we would have built into the system a bipper which would inform the patient in advance of an oncoming upheaval so that he might be prepared.

This advance beeping or bipping would be priceless to the man with the loose bowel. It would save him untoward emabarrassment should he be on the brink of a spate of diarrhoea.

These few sentiments and ideas should not be lightly dismissed. However, it is true to say that no two stomachs are alike. My grandfather who lived to be 93 drank a lot of whiskey in his life. Another man might have succumbed to such lethal doses at half that age.

Since no two stomachs are alike the distinction between stomachs must be identified and how better than through the system which I have suggested. Any time. Any time.

Question and Answers

FREQUENTLY AFTER a lecture the master of ceremonies asks the audience if they would like to put relevant questions to the lecturer. This is a sound idea but, alas, lurking in all audiences are persons male and female who are themselves well prepared to answer the questions they pose.

For years now I have been bored into semi-insensibility by these opportunistic predators. There I am, having contributed my quota of applause after the lecture has been concluded, in the act of pulling up my socks before departing when the MC falls into the age-old trap.

He may suggest that the questions should be pertinent and the answers brief so that the whole business might be concluded in a fifteen minute period. Alas there is no containing the man who would answer his own questions. He might not seem to be answering his own questions because he starts off by saying things like 'would not the lecturer agree' and follows up with a long dissertation which reveals all his personal philosophies. He will explain that under no circumstances would he be presumptuous enough to give a lecture himself but the simple truth is that he has a captive audience, albeit gathered in the first instance to listen to another. He is going to hold forth *ad nauseam* no matter how many times the MC may look at his watch.

I suggest that there should be a blacklist of these insufferable bores who have no regard for the feelings of others and whose only concern is that they unload their tedious vacuities on an audience too polite or too cautious to object. These brash buttonholers, and buttonholers they are, are forever on the lookout for inexperienced masters of ceremonies who foolishly presume that the rules they impose will be observed by all. Not even a tidal wave will halt a man who knows that it might well be years before he is provided with another opportunity.

On a number of occasions I have been obliged to play the role of chairman. Luckily I had a rogues' gallery of post-lectural criminals firmly framed in my mind's eye and I was able to ignore them by the simple expedient of pretending they didn't exist or by looking through them and afterwards apologising profusely when confronted with the accusation that I had deliberately ignored them.

'Never!' I would say in horror. I had no misgivings about such fabrications. I had a duty to the audience and I would protect them at all costs from being bored to tears. As a former victim myself it was my bounden duty to do so.

In appearance these lecture-hall miscreants are harmless and self-effacing. Apologetic is another word which occurs to me but given the slightest opening they can be ebullient and abrasive over long periods. It is the absolutely innocuous and gentle manner in which they lift an index finger to claim the MC's attention which is the most misleading and deceptive aspect of these seemingly harmless procrastinators. To the uninitiated MC here is a mild-mannered, easily-controlled dilettante who can be squatted like a fly if he persists beyond the allotted minutes. Believe me gentle reader once the scoundrel gets underway it would be easier for a group of old ladies to subdue an all-Black scrum.

A friend once suggested to me after we had been subjected to a question twenty minutes long that it might be a good idea to lock the speaker into a sound-proof room for a whole day and to replay for him at least forty times his own humourless outpourings.

Another alternative is to disallow all questions as soon

as the lecturer has finished thereby bringing merciful relief to those long-suffering souls who have suffered more than their share over a lifetime of lecturing.

Health

I HAVE been convinced for some time that good health abounds where a man has a good woman. I am blessed with relatively good health and I believe that I owe my condition to the ministrations of my spouse.

A nagging spouse as any hen-pecked husband or wife will affirm is a sure recipe for ulcers, sleeplessness, weight loss, teeth-grinding, frayed nerves and bad breath. Untold damage is done to both the appetite and the digestion and very often the victim can be heard nattering to itself. I knew a woman who used to hide herself in the wardrobe from her husband's tirades and I knew a man who used to go under the bed but not before he stuffed his ears with cotton wool.

I don't have to hear or see a man mincing with his molars to know that he is a teeth-grinder. I don't have to look into his eyes to see his anguish. All I have to do is listen to his wife for ten minutes. The same applies to a teeth-grinding wife. Teeth-grinding is damaging to the gums and reduces the consumption of saliva which is essential to the digestive tract. It seriously affects the hearing and contributes to slurry speech.

As I listen to the wife rasping or the man, as the case may be, I know after a short while how discontented she is with her lot and how resentful she is about the lots of others which she presumes, nearly always wrongly, are better than her own. The man at the receiving end of this woman's outpourings is certain to acquire poor health after a short space of time. This female's fables of discontent and her penchant for flinging non-stop verbal darts at her husband from every angle eventually transforms him into a teeth-grinder, then into a grinner and in the course of time into a candidate for a coffin.

Health abounds where there is a helpful spouse, Fat and gristle are annihilated under the influence of a husband or wife who wishes well to the opposite number.

God help the spouse whose partner never lets up on the abusive chatter. The very presence of such a partner is as dangerous to the digestive system as a frying pan which hasn't been washed in forty outings.

Ah but blessed is he who hath a loving and merry spouse! If he is benign it does not matter that she cannot cook because true love will disintegrate anything from gristle to sinew.

True love maketh the soapy spud floury and the burnt rashers sweet. True love maketh sour milk sweet and maketh bread without yeast to rise. True love maketh light of the beer-drinking of the spouse and is silent always during the morning after the night before and the morning after the morning of the night before. True love maketh watery gravy rich and tasty and it taketh away the lard and the grease and the grit and maketh the fare seem as the fare of princes. Here then in the presence of a good and helpful spouse is good health to be found. Seek not for it in the apothecary's bottle nor the doctor's prescription but search for it and make it your own where the smile killeth the frown and harmony dominates the scene as the rainbow after the storm.

One of the only great writers to concern himself with health was Izaak Walton. I have never read any observations by the other great writers concerning health. In fact I doubt if I have come across one sagacious comment about health in all my years of reading. This could well be that writers who are lucky enough to be possessed of good health take it for granted. Writers in general are pretty good grubbers and rarely turn their backs on intoxicating liquor. In fact most of the deceased writers I used to know were, as my mother used to say, martyrs to drink like our John.

But here is what Walton has to say: 'Look to your health and if you have it praise God and value it next to a good conscience for health is the second blessing, a blessing that money can't buy.'

How wrong was Walton! Health can be bought although not always. The wealthy were able to transport themselves to more favourable climes while the poor died at home of tuberculosis. Surely that is bought health.

In the end I am convinced that health and spousebliss go hand in hand. A benign spouse is the real cure for flatulence.

Fortune-Tellers of Old

FOTRTUNES ARE frequently told by simply looking at water in a basin. This form of forecasting is termed lecanomancy. Then there is the casting of bones or pebbles, the formation of which may be studied as soon as they fall to the ground.

An aunt of mine used to tell the future by looking at the tea leaves at the bottom of the cup used by the victim. Fortunes are told by the casting of cards and beware if you fall foul of the ace of spades or the ten of clubs!

The latter used to be called the 'Clare hearse' when I was a gorsoon. There are hundreds of systems whereby the future may be revealed but give me the palmist any day.

My first encounter with a palmist happened at Listowel Races many years ago. I had been after a lucky day at the races and was in a generous mood as I crossed the Island Bridge on my way to the nearest licensed premises. Suddenly, unexpectedly, I found my left hand resting gently in the right hand of a shawled female.

'Tell your fortune sir!' said she.

'Why not?' said I.

'Five bob,' said she.

'Half-a-crown,' said I. We eventually settled on three-and-sixpence.

'You'll cross water,' said she without batting an eyelid, 'and it won't be long.' She was dead right for starters because I had proposed earlier to visit the racecourse the following day which was the final day of the races. In order to do so I would have to cross the footbridge which spans the lovely river Feale and if that isn't crossing water I don't know what is.

'The world will wonder at your luck,' she said and how right she was there as well.

Then came ominous news. I knew by the look on her wrinkled, well-punished visage that calamity was in store for me.

'You'll fall out with a black-haired woman,' she said, 'and there will be ructions.'

I could afford to laugh this one off or so I believed but how right was that ancient fortune teller of yesteryear.

That night when I could drink no more, thoughts of home and my parents entered my head for the first time. I staggered from the square to my abode in the very heartland of Church Street, mecca of a hundred other drunks on that faraway occasion. The difference was, however, that I was not quite the legal age to qualify for the purchase of intoxicating liquor. Arriving home, I was pleased to discover that all was in darkness. I did a tiptoe up the stairs or what might be described as a drunken facsimile of a tiptoe. Alas, that same stairs was possessed and is still possessed of one creaky step to this very day. It gave me away and I was summoned into my parents' bedroom. All my other brothers had long left home so there was no escape by simply doubling back in the hope that somebody else would be blamed.

When I entered the room the light was on. My father was smoking his pipe as he read a novel and my mother's rosary lay limp across her palm. I don't know whether it was the tobacco smoke or the look on my mother's face but whichever it was I remember I fell across the bed and puked against the wall at the other side.

My mother turned purple and the lambasting began. Strips she peeled off me while all the time my father smoked his pipe and kept his own counsel.

The tinker woman had been right in each of her three prognostications. Her final one where she warned me about a black-haired woman was the truest. I thought at the time that she must have meant a girlfriend with black hair but I had no such girlfriend.

In fact I had no girlfriend at all. The black-haired woman was, of course, my poor mother, God grant her a bed in heaven. That was my first experience with a fortune-teller but it was not my last. It was the best value for money I ever got.

She had made three forecasts and each of the three was spot on and all for the miserly sum of three shillings and sixpence. Many people tend to dismiss the casual fortune-teller and pay more attention to prognosticators who practise in caravans and private rooms. Visits to these practitioners can be expensive while there is no guarantee that the forecasts are more accurate.

I once called to the caravan which housed a lady who went under the romantic title of Bella Rosa. I had a few drinks taken at the time and I had been commissioned by a newspaper to do a piece on palmistry and crystal gazing. The article never appeared and I'm not surprised because the first thing Bella Rosa told me was that I was in for a big disappointment.

'You gonna get da bigga let-down,' she warned. I was surprised by her accent because we often crossed paths in a public house in Cork and she always spoke as follows: 'Give us out two vods dere Cha. We have plinty white.'

The next thing Bella Rosa told me was that I would have a stroke of good luck in the near future. The consultation, by the way, took place a few days before the Munster football final.

'Does this mean,' I asked, 'that Kerry are going to beat Cork?'

'Corka!' she said and she laughed.

'Corka,' she repeated the word, and laughed even louder. 'Corka no beata Catty Barry,' she said, 'Corka is a fulla boloney.'

On the day, Kerry were five-to-one-on so I backed Cork at four-to-one-against. Bella Rosa had been right, Cork, on

103

the day, were a disaster. Ah but what changes since! Who would have believed on that distant, sunny afternoon that Cork would annihilate Kerry in the final of 1990? I asked her a final question.

'Who will win the all-Ireland final?' I asked.

'Daisa gonna be no final,' she made answer. I could not believe my ears. Time passed, and I was leaving Croke Park. Kerry had blotted out the Dubs, and there were surely heady times in the Kingdom. I met a relation of mine as I walked to my hotel.

'There was no final,' he said, 'there was a fiasco not a final.'

I thought about what Bella Rosa had told me. 'Daisa gonna be no final.' She was right. Three times out of three she had forecasted correctly and you'll hear people saying that fortune-telling is bunk, that it's all a racket.

My final visit to a fortune-teller was in Limerick. She shall be nameless. She carefully examined my palm before making a pronouncement. Let me say here that I made the visit, in the first place, while I was waiting for my wife who was buying a hat for a wedding. The fortune-teller had little to say except to caution me about a burning. There would, she said, be a fire which would affect my property.

Later in Limerick, I had a steak and one side was black from the burning it got. Need I say more about fortune-tellers?

Finely Wrought

AH THE Lord have mercy on the finely-wrought phrase! Supplanted now by the four letter word it is sorely missed. I remember commenting to a travelling man one time about the severity of the March weather. We met on a woodland path.

'It's bad,' I said.

'It's all right for the likes of us,' he said sadly, 'but it will do away with a lot of weak people.'

So it did, even people with heavy overcoats and dry boots, even people with three square meals a day, even people with warm fires and hot water bottles in their beds.

Then there was the time I was standing in the rain at a sparsely attended football game in Ballybunion. An elderly gentleman moved close in until we were both protected by my umbrella.

'Shocking weather!' I suggested.

'God help delicate people,' said he, 'for 'tis them that's in for it now.'

It was a variation on the tramp's observation and in that time and that place you could hear a hundred variations whereas now it all boils down to four letters.

Then there was the Cockney who came with me to Davy Gunn's abode in Derrindaffe. Davy is the great bodhrán-maker whose fame has rightly spread all over the world. We spoke about seasonal hides and so on.

'Beware the "'ides of March",' said the Cockney sagely, "'cos they make the worst bodhráns.'

Davy Gunn and his wife Maimie and myself were agreed that this man was one of our own.

Then there was the night of Listowel Races when a man who had never sung before made his debut with a hysterical interpretation of the hymn, 'O Salutaris!' The poor chap had spent the best part of his life in a mental institution. Neighbours and friends expressed alarm and concern at the phenomenon until the caretaker brother of the deranged man assured them that their fears were groundless.

'Don't worry,' said he, 'as soon as he gets back to normal he'll be out of his mind again.'

Then there was the night I arrived home drunk for the first time. I nearly made the journey from downstairs to upstairs without parental interference but then my father opened the bedroom door after hearing my step.

'A creaking step,' said he triumphantly, 'is as good as a dog and it eats very little, just a fragment of wax polish now and again.'

I once bought a drink in Tralee for a man who was recognised as the most professional and the most articulate drink cadger in the whole of Kerry. Then a lesser bum entered but he was told to leave by the bum-in-residence.

'Try that chap over there,' he suggested, indicating a most unlikely source of free booze.

'That fella has nothing,' the lesser bum complained.

'Listen my friend,' said the bum-in-residence, 'a drunken pauper, if his virtues are properly over-extolled and his ego pumped up with the wind of undeserved praise, can often be induced to buy a drink for his eulogist.'

Then there was an argument in the bar about the rights and wrongs of nude bathing. Some insisted that it was sinful while others maintained it was harmless. Then there spoke a sage of four score years, a scholarly fellow who had savoured the brine of the seven seas and felt the fury of the four winds.

'There is nothing wrong with nudity,' said he, 'the wrong is in the human mind for,' he continued, 'of all the world's vistas the female posterior is the most surpassing. Who will deny that in all its unclad glory it is the most intoxicating of all prospects!'

And what about this for a piece of advice to those who might be drawing blind pensions and are not blind at all?

'If,' said the great matchmaker Dan Paddy Andy, 'there is one man who don't look like a pensions' officer that man is a pensions' officer.'

A Time for Pos

SOME DAY somebody will write a comprehensive history, fully illustrated, about the chamber pot and about various vessels designed for other purposes which have been pressed into service as chamber pots.

While we are waiting for such an opus, I propose to entertain my readers with a chamber pot incident. Prospective compilers of chamber pot anthologies are welcome to avail of it free of charge.

A man we shall call Pol Po happened to be a cousin of mine.

Pol answered an advertisement one time for the posiion of night porter in a well-known hotel in Killarney. He had no experience but in his favour it must be said that staying up all night was no trouble to him provided there was drink involved.

As a night porter in a hotel he would be handling drink and as his mother said he would have the smell of it and that should keep him going till he'd be off duty.

Pol Po of course was not his real name but, since his kinfolk were humourless fellows not given to repartee, with some still alive, I propose to use the name Pol Po instead of the real one. These kinfolk speak with their fists instead of their mouths and, believe me, they articulate fluently. We do not wish to draw their ire. Hence Pol Po.

When Pol was informed, some weeks after his application, that the job was his, he packed his ancient suitcases of which there were two. In those days when suitcases were filled, it was common practice to tie hats and caps and boots to the outside with ropes or belts.

I remember well that Pol Po visited a neighbour's house before his departure. He came for the loan of a po.

The vessel was immediately forthcoming because the people to whose house he called would give a person their beds as well as their chamber pots so good-natured and well-intentioned were they towards their neighbours.

The po in question was a venerable one. It was made from tin and, although battered and dented, it was without a leak.

People should try to remember that it is not the scenic drawings on a po or the figarios attached to it that matter. Rather is it the lasting powers of the pot in question.

An enamel po will chip and an earthenware po will crack but a tin po will last forever if it is treated respectfully.

Our friend set out for Killarney unaware that the hotels there were full of water-closets and that under every bed was a pot of one kind or another. His po was firmly strapped to his suitcase as he made tracks for Beauty's Home.

When he arrived he found that the job was gone. He had arrived a week too late. It wasn't his fault. He had relied on his mother for the day and date. She was rarely right about such matters. Often it would be Monday when she'd start thinking of Sunday Mass.

Pol Po returned home with his bags intact. On the outside the tin po was still strapped. He was a sorry sight as he trudged up the street to his mother's house. She greeted him like the Prodigal Son. She spent the better part of her old age pension on some fatted bullock at a local butcher's so that his return from afar might be celebrated properly.

Never since that time did I see a man with a chamber pot strapped to his suitcase. I asked around and was told that it was common enough at the hiring fairs in the earlier part of the century. Spailpeens with irregular kidneys would often bring their own chamber pots along with them. These were often home-made but they were always serviceable.

In capable hands a bucket or a gallon could be transformed into a most presentable po. Tinkers thought nothing of dashing off six or seven reliable tin pots in the space of an hour. Pos were never stolen. To steal a man's po in the west of Ireland was the same as stealing a man's horse in Texas. Swift and terrible retribution followed.

Before I close, just as a matter of historical interest, there were no plastic pos in that distant time. The arrival of plastic brought the po within every man's reach. By no means as grand as its more ornate counterpart nor half as musical, it played its primary role efficiently and that, after all, is what matters in the end.

Let me say too that it was common enough for itinerant thatchers, tailors and shoemakers to bring along their chamber pots when working in distant houses.

Those of these esteemed trades who fancied a few beers before retiring owe much to the travelling po.

Weird Words

SOMETIMES I like to think I am a refugee from the kingdom of Humdrum whose ruler is King Prosaic. I have no choice in the matter when conversation in the pub turns away from the pedestrian. This happens only on certain afternoons. The afternoon attracts a certain kind of drinker who is given to conversation and observations out of the ordinary.

One Wednesday an afternoon tippler who happens to be a retired educator addressed himself to a countryman sitting close by in particular and to the three other customers in general.

'There are a lot of unfortunate words,' said he 'in need of exercise! Such as gotra and xenodochium and johablanca.'

'Are they really there?' asked Davy Gunn the bodhrán-maker who happened to be sitting near the window.

'Oh yes,' said the teacher 'they are there all right.'

'What's the longest word in the world?' asked a farmer from Ballybunion.

'The longest word in the world is boredom,' the teacher replied. Davy Gunn nodded in agreement.

'And the shortest word?' ask the farmer.

'I have no interest in short words,' the teacher responded testily, 'let us give words like the ones I mentioned a chance.'

'Hallelujah!' exclaimed Davy Gunn.

'Give that man whatever he's drinking,' said the teacher and he beamed upon the bodhrán-maker as though he was a prize-pupil.

'You're not biased,' he said to Gunn, 'you give words a chance.'

'Cock-a-doodle-doo!' said Davy Gunn.

'I know now,' said a Waterford man, an elderly commercial who likes to hop balls, 'why Kerry won so many All-Ireland finals.'

Dead silence ensued. Could there be another reason in addition to all the other ones which had already been trotted out for so long.

'It's the colours,' said the Waterford commercial. 'It took me a long time to figure but I got it in the end. It's the colours.'

Looks were exchanged. We had heard them all and here was a span new one concocted by a Decies man.

'Green and gold are the colours you will find in any football field in the land, mostly green I'll grant you but the suggestion of yellow is always there especially in late September which is All-Ireland time and when there's a tinge of gold in the grasses. The opposition just cannot see the Kerryman coming. That's how they got all those soft goals. The backs and the goalie were unsighted as the Kerry forwards blended in with the natural colours of the pitch. They seemed to come out of the ground. They were part of the background whereas the blue of the Dubs was plainly visible.'

A long silence ensued, 'Is there a word for that sort of thing?' Davy Gunn asked the teacher.

'Yes,' said he of the books 'the word is bias, unintentional bias but bias nevertheless and it is a commodity which every man born of woman possesses in varying degrees and if we would only admit to it the world would be a better place.'

The Waterford man firmly believed that he was speaking the truth but his case would hardly stand up in court because there are other counties who wear green and gold and they haven't won as many All-Irelands as Kerry. Still the Decies man made his point and who knows but there might be an element of truth in it.

'I daresay I'm committing felo de se when I utter such sacrilegious talk in Kerry,' said he.

'What is felo de se?' asked a small man who had not spoken up to this point.

'Felo de se,' said the teacher, 'is a fellow from the sea or if you like a chap from Ballybunion just like that man over there.'

Female Wrongs

IN RECENT times there has been no scarcity of radio and television programmes concerning the victimisation of the female of the species, concerning the reluctance of the male of the species to involve himself in household work, concerning his willingness to participate in all meals and his unwillingness to participate in the washing up. There's no doubt but that he has gotten away with murder for generations.

Let me be among the first to say *mea culpa*. With ninety-nine percent of the male population of the Republic of Ireland I plead guilty to the crime of non-participation in household chores except on very rare occasions when the woman of the house was indisposed. The only defence I can offer is that after initial efforts to render assistance I was thereafter never encouraged to take part. I was accused of doing more damage than good and wrongfully accused of doing so deliberately in order to avoid involvement in such goings-on in the future.

I will concede however that there are many glaring injustices being perpetrated against the Irish female and if I have been guilty in the past I hereby resolve never to be guilty in the future.

Bad as we are in respect of victimisation of the female we are only trotting after our ancestors. When I was a gorsoon it was unthinkeable for a woman to present herself in a licensed premises unless she was on the warpath after a drunken husband who had neglected to carry home his wages and was content to see his wife and children starve so long as he could fill his gut with porter. Even then women were frowned upon and the one thing, acceptable to male customers and male barmen, was to send in a child to tell

114

the offending wretch that he was wanted at home.

I remember too being astonished to hear cluck-clucks of disapproval when a woman wearing a black shawl went up the centre aisle of the church. Fine if she went up the side aisles or remained at the rear of the church. Bad, however, as these sins against women were at the time there were far worse. Women were supposed to eat less and were expected to decline offers of strong drink when offered same. It was fine for men to drink but not fine for women.

One outstanding case of bias against women I will never forget. It was during the twelve o'clock mass many, many years ago. There was always a long sermon in those days, a long rambling sermon that most massgoers could make neither head nor tail of. It went on and on and on until half the congregation was either asleep or dozing. Then came the announcement out of the blue that the man in the pulpit had been shocked out of his ecclesiastical wits only a few short days before.

There he was, passing through the town square when he beheld a woman staggering in front of him. When she fell to the ground he went to her assistance and was astonished to find that she was drunk. He raised a finger of admonition to the congregation and there was a silence in the church the like of which I personally had never experienced before.

'A drunken man, after all,' he said, 'is only a drunken man but a drunken woman is a drunken woman.'

He stressed the words 'drunken woman' and one got the distinct impression that a drunken dog was a noble creature by comparison. He forgot to mention that there had been drunken men falling about the streets of the town since the opening of its first tavern. In fact I once wrote about the longest drunken stagger I had ever seen. I have long been a student of drunken staggers and it totally eclipsed all others for length and misdirection. It was of course executed by a man, a drunken man. Up until that time I had never seen a woman stagger but they were the more culpable, drinkwise, in the eyes of the clergy.

'Frailty,' wrote Shakespeare, 'thy name is woman'. Alas poor Shakespeare. He should know better than any that the only thing frailler than a woman is a man. Even I know that and I'm no Shakespeare.

Even Milton erred in his attitude towards the English female: 'Wisest men have erred and by bad women been deceived'. Surely he knew that men are the acknowledged deceivers and for every woman who deceived a man there are a hundred men who deceived women.

When I was growing up and even still a woman of the house never sat to table until every other member had been seated first. When did we ever see a man on his knees scrubbing a floor? When I see it I'll eat the scrubbing brush.

Fame

I AM reminded again of what Frances Bacon said of fame. 'Fame,' said he, 'is like a river. It will bear up that which is light and swollen but will sink that which is weighty and solid.'

They may not be the exact words but the gist is there. Then we have Milton's observation on fame:

> Fame is the spur that the clear spirit doth raise
> That last infirmity of noble mind
> To scorn delights and live laborious days
> But the fair guerdon when we hope to find
> And think to burst out into sudden blaze
> Comes the blind fury with the abhorred shears
> And slits the thin-spun life.

Alas and alack how woefully and hurtfully true for that is, indeed, the way with life.

Speaking a few years ago on 'The Late Late Show' about fame I overlooked a few important aspects of this mercurial commodity, this glitsy varnisher of unfortunate mortals, this crucifier of those who would withdraw peacefully and husband out life's taper at the close as the poet said, husband it out somewhere where the wind wouldn't blow it out.

There was once a famous man in this part of the world. At least he was better known than most. He was an outgoing chap who made lasting impressions on people from other parts of the country, good impressions mostly for he was a good singer, a good raconteur, a fairly good athlete and an excellent sportsman.

As the years progressed his fame grew but because of

his travels his purse lightened until a sad day came when he found himself without financial resources of any kind. He wasn't in debt fortunately; he wasn't that kind of fellow.

It so happened that during the earlier days of his impecuniosity he found himself on his way home from a football game with a party of friends. He stopped at a pub where he had been in the habit of stopping for years and when his turn to buy a round of drinks came he discovered that he had not the wherewithal to meet his obligation. Discreetly he called the woman of the house aside and explained that he was a trifle short but that he would be in town the next pig market when he would settle his account after disposing of two pigs which he was fattening.

'We don't go in for that sort of thing at all,' said the woman of the house and without another word of explanation she devoted her attention to a more prosperous customer. Our friend realised for the first time that his kind of fame was worthless. It was not an exchangeable asset. In short it could not be realised into anything of substance.

Realising his plight one of his friends insisted upon paying for the round but this wasn't the same thing at all. The fun was knocked out of it when our friend discovered that his word wasn't to be honoured and this, to him, was the great setback of his life. It changed his whole outlook for several years until one night he came to see a production of Patrick Kavanagh's *Tarry Flynn* as adapted for the stage by the late and great P.J. O'Connor of Radio Éireann.

Afterwards he spoke to me in a public house contiguous to the theatre and expressed his satisfaction with the production. He rubbed his hands with delight and then shook hands with the producer and with the cast.

'Bless you one and all,' he said, 'bless you, bless you, bless you.'

None of us had ever before felt so totally gratified at

the conclusion of any performance such was his genuine approbation.

'I am a new man,' he said. 'I was down but now I am up and I shall not be down again'.

'What aspect of the play changed you?' I asked. He was quick to explain but in order to clear his throat he invested in a half glass of whiskey the better to ready his larynx for its contribution.

'You remember,' said he, 'the part of the play where Paddy McNamee was going to town happy and carefree?'

I nodded that I did.

'You remember,' said he, 'how he heard the blackbird singing "Spend, spend and God will send"?'

I nodded that I did. 'Well,' he said, 'wasn't I just like that?'

He then went on to recall what the blackbird sang as Paddy McNamee was returning home drunk and broke from the town.

'Have it yourself,' the blackbird sang, 'or be without it.'

That then was our friend's turning point. He knew that Paddy McNamee and Paddy Kavanagh had gone through the same mill. The moral here is that fame won't buy you a drink and it certainly won't get you into heaven.

Then there's the quatrain from Longfellow's 'Psalm of Life':

Lives of great men all remind us
We can make our lives sublime
And departing leave behind us
Footprints on the sands of time.

I discussed this very extract several years ago with a distant relation who had, like many another deluded gorsoon, great expectations of his father who was regarded locally as a famous man and in this instance probably a great man. He died and was waked and was buried. Nobody could deny his right to heaven for he had never been a man of the world and also he was tolerant and charitable to a fault.

'Blasht him,' said the son, 'he didn't leave me as much as would buy a box of matches.'

'He left you his good name,' I argued and then I went on to quote from Longfellow's poem.

'Footprints!' he said scornfully.

'In the sands of time,' I said hopefully.

'What will the bank manager give me,' said he bitterly, 'for footprints in the sands of time?'

'You're missing the point,' I told him.

'I'll tell you what,' he said. 'Since you set such store by these footprints I'll give them to you for the price of a pair of shoes.'

That finished the argument. However, a moral remains. Ninety-nine point nine percent of people would rather a legacy of cash than a legacy of honour. It's sad but true and alas it's the way of the world.

'It's not negotiable', a man said to me once on the Tralee road when I thanked him profusely for helping me change a wheel on a wet day. I had no money on me. When I asked him for his name and address he explained that it wasn't money he wanted but rather had the world made him sick of superfluous thanks.

In my childhood there was a commodity called a 'God spare you the Health Cheque' which was given by mean people to workers instead of common cash. The way I look at it, it was a lot better than no thanks at all and certainly a lot better than a curse!

Medical Mix-Up

MOST OF my male customers have become greatly perturbed of late and the cause is a report which has appeared in a number of newspapers. It is a matter of some delicacy and it is with considerable reluctance that I raise it at all. In the public interest I feel that it must not be swept under the table. My detractors, of course, with characteristic lack of objectivity, will say that I am obsessed with matters relating to sex. This is quite untrue. I have written more about corner boys than sex. I have even written more about dogs than I have about sex. However, I am prepared to concede that those under the age of three should not read this contribution.

Apparently recent medical research, by certain doctors, has shown that a man who drinks an average of two pints of stout per night will suffer from sexual decline of the most serious nature after a prescribed period. In fact, the study claims that the nether area of the human rooster will become 'shrivelled up' and disappear altogether! May I hasten to add, at this stage, that nobody was more alarmed than myself by what I read. The inverted words are the doctors', not mine!

As always, however, I decided to throw the matter open for discussion among my clients before repairing posthaste for medical advice. The first man to speak was a veteran of fifty-one years marital confrontation, an old-age pensioner from Ballylongford. I told him of the revelations concerning one of man's more cherished areas.

Said he: 'Every night of my life for the past forty years I have drunk five pints of stout and a few halves of whiskey and my wife will tell you that I'm the most fervent buck in Ballylongford.'

"'Tis me that knows it,' said the lady in question who happened to be present. 'The only rest I get is when he goes off the drink.'

Said a man from Tarbert: 'Bring these doctors here and let them go forth amongst the pint drinkers of North Kerry and they'll go home with a different story. I'm sixty-six years of age and although I never married there is no woman in Tarbert would trust me alone in a room with her. There is no day I don't drink three to four pints and no night I don't drink three or four more. I never went home drunk and I never went home without having a mind for women.'

'Week after week,' said a man from Ballybunion, 'we read these stories from doctors. One week they're warning us about eating too much fat and another week about eating too much lean. I'm seventy-seven and I always ate according to my fancy and drank my fill of whiskey and there is no ram between here and Portmagee would lace my boots.'

'That's right,' said the Ballylongford man. 'If we was to believe them doctors we'd all die of starvation. You'll read of one fellow saying that liver is bad for you and another that liver is good for you. I had three brothers that was very fond of fish and the three of them are dead these twenty years. I never looked at as much as a sprat and I'll surely do the hundred.'

'I think there's a lot of 'em gone in the head,' said the Tarbert man. 'Imagine to go saying that a man who drinks a few pints is going to be deprived of his faculties! You wouldn't hear it in a lying competition.'

The debate went on and the conclusion that was reached was this:

Some form of medical authority should be organised which would have special responsibility for the vetting of the more ludicrous outpourings of the medical fraternity. Extensive damage to an already-harassed licensing trade would seem to be inevitable unless some steps are taken.

Already in Listowel at the time of writing at least five males have gone off the drink but one man put it rather conversely in another pub when he was asked if he proposed to go off the booze because of the alleged danger to his sex life.

'I'm past fifty-five,' he said, 'and I'd have to think about it very carefully before deciding one way or the other.'

In the end, under pressure, he vowed that he would go off the drink.

'Typical!' said an unattached female who happened to be within earshot.

At the end of the our public house deliberations it was the consensus of opinion that future pronouncements of sexual matters by members of the medical profession should be taken with a grain of sodium chloride and swallowed down with a tablespoonful of *aqua pura*.

Poor Relations

It is a melancholy truth that even great men have their poor relations.

DICKENS

WHEN MISFORTUNE smites the poor they have nowhere to turn but to their rich relations. When I was young I had no rich relations. A few were well off all right but the remainder were like ourselves, up one day and down the next.

The tragedy is that there aren't enough rich relations to go round. While I have no figures at my fingertips I think I would be safe in saying that for every rich relation there are twenty poor ones. Maybe there are more. Only those who are very rich could say for sure.

This puts a lot of pressure on rich relations and because of this they are always on the defensive. They are obliged to manufacture a wide stock of ready-made answers such as: 'Every penny I have is tied up' or 'my overdraft is sky high as it is'.

Other ploys resorted to by rich relations are to be abject in appearance and poor of mouth or to surprise the borrower by trying to borrow from him first.

For lesser appeals such as the price of a drink or the loan of a fiver there is the rituaListic turning out of the trousers pockets to show that the besieged party has nothing on him. Another useful trick is to hand over a wallet with nothing in it, at the same time telling the victim that he can keep all the money he finds in it.

For large amounts something more effective is required such as a visible feeling of concern for the problems of the would-be borrower.

I was in the kitchen of a farmer's house one time when a poor relation called in search of a substantial sum of money. He required it to pay a fine and compensation for an offence committed while under the influence. If the money was not forthcoming it was certain that he would wind up in jail which, in his view, meant that not only himself but also his relations would be disgraced in the eyes of the countryside.

'My friend,' said the farmer, 'if I had money you would have no need to call because knowing your plight I would hand it over without being asked. Would you believe,' the farmer went on as he took a large cigarette packet from his pocket, 'that this is my last fag. God only knows where the price of the next one is to come from.'

So saying he threw the empty box on the floor, placed the cigarette in his mouth, bent o'er the fire, lifted a coal, blew on it, applied it to the cigarette and was soon puffing contentedly as he calmly awaited the next cue in what to him was a comedy but to his visitor a tragedy.

'You could sell a cow,' said the poor relation. 'You wouldn't miss one and I swear I'd pay you back before the end of the year.'

'Of course I could sell a cow,' said the farmer, 'and if you got into trouble again I could sell another cow. Word would spread and any time a relation was in trouble I could sell a cow but what would I do when the cows were all gone? People would ask me why did I sell all my cows when I'd ask them for help.'

The poor relation held his tongue at this rebuff while the farmer shook his head at the injustice of it all.

'I would have nowhere to turn,' he said with a tear in his eye.

I almost shed a tear myself as I listened. At first I had been sorry for the poor relation. Now I was even sorrier for the farmer. There was a contorted look of sheer weariness on his face. He looked wanly into the fire before he spoke again.

'I have nowhere to turn,' he choked as though his cows were sold already. 'I have no well-off relations like others. All my relations are poor. They haven't a penny to put on top of another. You wouldn't like to see me pauperised would you? You wouldn't want to see me with a bag on my back walking the roads?'

Here the farmer laid a hand on the shoulder of his poor relation. He looked him in the eye for several seconds.

'Of course you wouldn't,' he answered in the poor fellow's stead, 'because you're not that kind of a man. You know what it's like to have nothing yourself and you wouldn't like to see another in the same fix, especially one of your own.'

After the poor relation had departed the farmer produced a large packet of Gold Flakes from another pocket, ripped off the protective tissue and extracted a cigarette which he lit from the expiring butt of the first.

Clouds

JUST STANDING in a country bohareen or a riverside or a field or a hillside looking upwards at the sky can be a truly lovely experience especially if the scene overhead is graced with clouds.

It is better to look all around and into the distance if the sun shines for the sun heightens and sharpens every aspect of the landscape. However, if there are clouds about, the upward look is the look for me. How's that Shelley puts it about the cloud?

> *I wield the flail of the lashing hail*
> *And whiten the green plains under*
> *And then again I dissolve it in rain*
> *And laugh as I pass in thunder.*

Of course, there are gentler, more billowing clouds which drift gently onwards, never releasing a drop. It takes all kinds to make up a comprehensive sky, the billowing as well as the blustering.

As I stood looking at the late autumn sky recently, a skein of wild duck passed overhead. They were low-flying at the time so that the deep whir of the fanning wings was audible for a brief period. It was a priceless experience because the whirring of so many duck wings in the same area is a blessed rarity indeed.

Wing-whirring of all kinds is extremely refreshing and if one is fortunate enough to be in the countryside when massive flights of starlings fly head-high homewards in the evenings it is a most engaging encounter. Then there are the whispering whirrings of finches whose bobbing flights are a constant delight.

As I stood raptly in mute adoration a large man barked into my ear and made me leap out of my shoes almost. I had not noticed his arrival and indeed a man had never approached me in this spot before because it is situated in the very heart of Dirha Bog where humans are few and visiting ducks far outnumber visiting townies. I had not seen this particular person up to this time which made the sense of shock even greater.

'You're very quiet!' was the shattering observation he had made and to this very hour my right ear wilts when I recall the noise. His statement did not require an answer so I made no sound in the forlorn hope that he had said all he was going to say and that he would continue on into the bog and leave me to my study of the sky which was in a particularly changeable mood on the occasion. I smiled benignly at him and he smiled back, looking upwards as he did to where my gaze had been concentrated.

He expected to see something highly unusual and was disappointed when his search revealed nothing but a mixture of grey and steel and clouds of a darker hue. I decided to speak.

'Fine selection,' I elected, pointing upwards to where a tidy gathering of dark greys stood dejected like a silent crowd waiting for a last minute goal from a football team whose performance had not equalled their expectations.

The man frowned and it was plain to be seen that while he was no hater of clouds he could take them or leave them. It was evident that they had made no great impact in his life so far, that his only concern was whether they were hail-filled or rain-filled.

Most people blame clouds for dispensing unwanted rain or hail which can have a decidedly wetting effect when accompanied by a strong gale. They never blame the faulty memories which induced them to forget their umbrellas. The reason I resented the intrusion of the ear-drum shatterer in the first place was out of my regard for clouds of all shapes and sizes. I am a cloud person and I am certain that there are others reading this contribution who are cloud persons too.

'The clouds,' said Yeats, 'have bundled up their heads high over Knocknarea' and is there anything as artistic as a nice bundle of white clouds at the end of a blue sky towards close of day?

Clouds keep presenting themselves day after day in varying colours, shapes and sizes. At no charge whatsoever do they transform themselves like enchanters from frazzled shapes impossible to interpret until they have assumed the fearsome bodies of lions and tigers and even dragons, in fact the shape of any monster or animal which man can imagine.

Clouds are best when they change into the larger animals like elephants or mighty mammals like whales. Then too they can appear as giant, grizzly heads on gigantic shoulders. I have seen clouds more human than humans and more animal than animals.

'Will you have a drink?' my tormentor was asking. The nearest pub was two and a half miles away. I declined on the grounds that I never drank till after nine at night, weddings, football matches and assorted outings excepted. How often on my way way home from such occasions, nicely sozzled, have I admired the lighter pastels of the heavenly clouds. Even cumbersome clouds are beautiful.

He followed my gaze again to where it had directed itself towards a sombre gathering of dark, bulbous, ominous rain-clouds which had replaced the previous tenants of the area under observation.

These newcomers reminded me of nothing but a cluster of penitents who are brimming over with tensions and turmoil until they can shrive themselves. The clouds above began to shrive themselves at that moment of drenching rain which suddenly came down upon our upturned faces without fear or favour. It was a good, honest rain that truly meant business.

It seemed to say: 'Go on away home now and let me get on with my business which is preserving the bloom on the face of nature.'

'Do you want a lift?' I enquired. He rubbed the rain into his face and then into his hair with podgy hands and seemed to savour it.

'Naw,' he replied, 'it's only a shower' and with that he moved off bogwards with his head in the air. It rained for several hours after that, heavy, consistent, uncom-promising rain which would be a boon to the rivers and the streams and the waterfalls and the ducks which had passed earlier and even to my friend, the ear-shatterer, that's if he was a rain person which I suspect he was.

I prayed that he wouldn't meet up with thunder clouds for they are preceded by dangerous flashes. Let us turn to Shelley once again who excels in his observations of all kinds of clouds:

> Sublime on the towers of my skiey bowers
> Lightning my pilot sits
> In a cavern under is fettered the thunder
> It struggles and howls at fits.

And how true is one of his prime comments on the cloud. No more need be said after this is said:

> I am the daughter of earth and water
> And the nursling of the sky
> I pass through the pores of the ocean and shores
> I change but I cannot die.

Funeral-Lovers

AROUND THIS part of the world the business of attending funerals takes precedence over all other forms of outdoor activity. Your average North Kerry funeral-goer will attend at least one hundred funerals per annum. Quite a substantial number will far exceed this quota while the out-and-out funeral addict will fret and fume if the mortality rate does not assure him of at least one funeral every day.

The addict will attend funerals whether he knows the deceased or not. For my own part I never like to go to funerals unless the deceased is known to me or is in some way related to me. I have a friend, however, who is forever on the outlook for funerals.

Every morning he purchases the daily paper for no other purpose than to scan the death page in the hope of finding details of a local funeral. Now you wouldn't mind if he was a businessman. It would be natural for him to seek out the relatives of the deceased in order to tell them how sorry he was. As a consequence the next time the relatives in question arrived in town they would seek out the businessman who had presented himself at the funeral and repay the man's concern by making a purchase in his establishment.

Our friend, however, has no business of any kind. When he arrives home with his newspaper he dons his spectacles and, ignoring the front and back pages, proceeds to peruse the death notices with the utmost assiduity. His day is made if there is a local death announced. His day is doubly made if there are two deaths. If there is no local death he will take it out on his unfortunate wife.

He was once accused by a neighbour of having nothing

to do except draw his pension. He recoiled in anger at the injustice of the observation. Raving and ranting he pointed out that he had his funerals.

'We buried Jack Moules this morning,' he said proudly, 'and we'll be taking Maggie Flavin to the chapel this evening.'

My beloved wife and the woman who works for us are both funeral addicts. Every day the woman who works for us buys her own paper apart from those I buy. She buys it solely for the purpose of reading the death notices. This in itself is good, even commendable, as long as I am left out of it. I have been forced to fix a personal quota of funerals if I am not to be on the move to and from burials and funeral parlours all year long. I will always attend the funeral of a friend or relative but I cannot be expected to be present at the obsequies of every Tom, Dick and Harry. It is the opposite with my wife and the woman who works for us. When they discover a local death a new sense of urgency and purpose enters into the business of the day. They no longer express shock and surprise when I opt out and tell them that they are free to go themselves but under no circumstances must they expect me to go.

There have been times after a hasty perusal of the death notices when I have been obliged to conceal the paper. I only stoop to this when my funeral quota has been filled and when the deceased is only half-known to me. If I were to take the course normally followed by the females of the household I would never get anything done and the greater part of my life would be devoted to mourning.

The ruse of hiding the newspapers no longer works because nowadays when they cannot find them they put two and two together and gird themselves for a funeral. Somebody who is aware of their commitment to the dead will be sure to inform them of the most recent death before the day is out. This proclivity towards funeral-going would seem to be frivolous but for the fact that the subject is basically serious.

I remember one time a young bank clerk complained in a public house in Listowel that there was nothing to do.

'You must be mad,' said the publican's wife, 'isn't there a funeral every day of the week!'

Such a proceleusmatic direction to one so young should normally fall on deaf ears but the truth of the matter is that he started to go to funerals and when last I enquired about him I heard, alas, that he had been the centrepiece of a funeral himself, one of the biggest ever seen and why not! He had himself never missed a funeral in the town where he eventually became bank manager.

I am not suggesting for a moment that those who dominate the funeral scene in this part of the world do so for the want of something better to do. They funeralise because it's a way of life and maybe at the backs of their minds there is a hidden fear that if they don't go to funerals regularly then, horror of horrors, nobody might show up at their own.

Tear-Jerkers

MOST MEN shed maybe a gallon of tears in a lifetime with the average woman shedding about three times that amount.

I am basing my figures on the tear density of an average cry which I reckon to be about one eighteenth of an ounce. I arrived at this moment from drawing upon the personal experiences of myself and others.

To find out the amount of liquid contained in an average cry, my method is to weigh the handkerchief used to absorb the tears before and after the cry and then subtract one from the other.

Alas there are no universally scientific returns available so that it is possible that my figures may not be all that accurate. In the absence of better, however, we shall have to go along with them for the present.

There is a tearful line to be found in *As You Like It.* Correct me if I'm wrong:

> *The big round tears*
> *Coursed one another down his innocent nose*
> *In piteous chase.*

Big round tears must not always be taken seriously. I would imagine myself that small, spattery tears contain infinitely more grief and that all tears, no matter how big or how abundant, do not always indicate true grief.

Every community has its tear-spiller who will cry at the drop of a hat. Their tear sources are always easily tappeable and there are many women whose lifetime output of tears could be measured in barrels rather than gallons.

In fact, there is one of my acquaintance whose tear-flow

so far could be measured in vats but then she cries at everything from Holy Communions to Confirmations, from births to deaths to stage plays and television films. It would appear that she has an inexhaustible supply of tears which is a very useful thing especially at a funeral where the chief mourners are either unwilling or unable to cry. Here she can act as a tear-leader.

'She has enough tears shed to float the *Queen Mary*,' I heard the expression many years ago as I left a graveyard after an old lady of the neighbourhood was laid in her resting place.

The man who spoke was referring to a lady who stood comforting the deceased's relatives at the graveyard gate. She was tear-stained all over and every so often she would indulge in another bout. This was all right in itself for she was a professional crier.

The tragedy was that she was also a tear-jerker and succeeded in inducing excess tears from people who had already cried their fill. The innocent reader may feel like intervening here to say that a few extra tears will make no great difference. Ah my dear reader, should we not know by now that in this world moderation in all things is the greatest of all guidelines.

When a person is forced by a tear-jerker to shed more tears than are strictly necessary some other part of the anatomy is sure to be deprived of the water that has been called up to manufacture the extra tears. A nose can dry up with disastrous consequences and then we have parched lips and wrinkled gums, not to mention dryness of the mouth and throat. Who has not heard of dry skin? Are not the newspapers and television stations forever advertising creams, liquids and what have you as curatives whereas one of the major causes all along may well have been the discharge of too many tears.

I have female friends who tell me that they dread going out of doors after the loss of a relative. So numerous are the tear-jerkers they meet during shopping expeditions that they return home quite tearless and complaining of headaches. What has happened is that certain necessary waters have been drained away from the head so that the inside of the skull heats up and gives rise to unprecedented headaches.

These tear-jerkers have plenty of liquid in the head's interior themselves so that they never suffer headaches. They lie in wait at street corners and outside busy shops waiting to pounce on an unfortunate woman who has suffered some form of misfortune.

A sympathetic look or the mere squeeze of a hand is enough to trigger off a stream of tears which the victim can ill afford. A kind word will do just as nicely to produce the drops which may well be leaving the victim's head an arid and dangerous place which may well crack before the natural water returns to fill up the tear-reservoirs which have become dried by the hypocritical or even well-meaning ministrations of the tear-jerker.

It is imperative therefore, for those who have suffered tragedy to avoid all tear-jerkers for a period of at least a year until the grief has been partially eroded by the passage of time.

The Weather

ALL LAST week I was subjected to observations and questions regarding the weather. People would ask me if I thought the rain would stop or continue, knowing that I was as ignorant of the meteorological scene as they were themselves.

If the professional weather forecasters of radio and television are sometimes fallible what price an amateur like me who can only forecast rain when he finds the first drop on his forehead.

'Do you think it will rain?' they would ask anxiously and await my prognostication in the desperate hope that I would answer in the negative.

In my home town of Listowel since I was a boy it was always believed that rain would fall whenever dark clouds appeared over the Listowel Arms Hotel. More often than not it does indeed rain when these ominous clouds appear.

Then there was Moran's dog who always crossed to the other side of the street prior to a heatwave. He erred once when he crossed over to interrogate a passing bitch. He was never forgiven.

Forecasting is mightily important to farmers and those dependant on fine or foul weather but talking about the weather is a different kettle of fish. What I mean is making inane pronouncements the likes of 'it's very wet' or 'it's very cold'.

Those to whom these facts are revealed are already well aware that it's wet or warm or cold so that there's really no need to tell them. In short it's a waste of time and that is why I would ask that a government embargo be placed on all such pointless pronouncements.

I would ask that modest fines be imposed in the early stages while offenders were getting used to the new law. Then in the course of time, for persistent offenders, I would like to see heavier fines imposed. Ultimately, however, for habitual weather criminals I feel they should be made to involve themselves in work which would benefit the community such as planting rose bushes and shrubs where the briar and nettle rule the roost. They might also be made to eradicate eyesores and to generally beautify, without monetary recompense, all places which offend the on-looker's senses.

This, I believe, would greatly improve the standard of general conversation. Without recourse to the weather the man on the street would be obliged to use his imagination for a change and make pronouncements which could well improve the human situation. Instead of remarking how fine the day is a person might say for instance 'What this country needs is to grow all of its own cauliflowers' or 'Go home and till your wasteland.'

These are the sort of sensible observations which make people conscious of the need to improve the national output. Even if only one in ten people heeded the advice tendered look at the dramatic reduction you would have in the import of cauliflowers and the massive development of neglected gardens and plots which could be made to produce more food.

I am not suggesting for a minute that there should be an immediate and permanent ban on weather observations which are already well known. You cannot change a habit which is tens of thousand of years in existence but you can make a beginning.

First an advance warning of say a year should be given with huge advertisements in all of our newspapers, televisions and radio. There should be public debates on the matter and, of course, it would have to be thoroughly de-bated in the government chambers before a bill could be put through. Then when people are fully prepared the bill should become law. Automatically the number of poets in the country would be doubled. The latent poetry which is in all of us would certainly be stimulated by our having to resort to more colourful outpourings than unrewarding comments on the state of the weather.

The standard of conversation and debate would immediately lift itself above the pedestrian and when we would come in from the streets our ears would be ringing with the beauty and sharpness of the phrases to which they had been subjected by hitherto inarticulate friends and neighbours. With the weather out of the way there need be no limit to the scope and quality of the new messages man must inevitably formulate. Men would vie with each other in the colour and depth of their disclosures.

Let me conclude by saying to the cynic and the negator that we must not ignore any opportunity, no matter how outrageous it might seem, that might better the world we live in. *Quod semper, Quod ubique, Quod ab omnibus.*

Umbrellas

I WISH I had an umbrella. Next to 'please close that door' it must surely be one of the most oft-repeated statements in the vocabulary of man.

I didn't realise, however, until quite recently that umbrellas make strange bedfellows.

Often in the past I had given the shade of my umbrella to all manner of man. Religion, politics or sex never entered into it but unconsciously I had been sharing my shade with men and women with whom I would not normally pass the time of day or enter into any form of relationship. This is good and for this reason alone I would ask more people to use umbrellas.

I mean if you haven't got an umbrella you cannot share it and if you cannot share it your chances of establishing new relationships are likely to be restricted.

My awakening to the true role of umbrellas came recently at a funeral. The deceased had been a harmless fellow in life and now, in death, was at the height of his popularity. How popular is he who is safely dead and who has been scratched from the entry sheet! Now may we at last shower him with affection and withhold no longer his full due of encomiums.

As we parked our cars a long distance from the funeral home where the mortal remains were on display the clouds overhead began to spill their cargoes. Those who had brought hats and caps thanked their stars but those who had brought umbrellas commended themselves endlessly and effusively.

How wise is he who never forgets his umbrella! Only he who has been drenched over and over manages to acquire such wisdom and even then the wisest may still forget.

One of the most chastening and bitter experiences is when one recognises one's own umbrella in the hands of another. It happened once to myself but I held my tongue. A lost umbrella can be replaced, a lost lawsuit never. I forget who the poet was to whom we are indebted for the following perceptive stanza: —

The rain it raineth on the just
And also on the unjust fella
But chiefly on the just because
The unjust steals the just's umbrella

Not all umbrellas have been stolen, of course. Some have been found and others borrowed.

As we hurried to the funeral home, a few fortunate mourners were offered shades by the proprietors of the roomier umbrellas. They were accepted with alacrity and thus were established relationships between lawmen and criminals, rich men and poor men, ignorant and educated, conservative and subversive, laymen and clergymen, between the thin and the fat, the short and the tall, the bald and the curly.

It was not the rain that brought them together. We've always had rain but we had to wait for the umbrella in order that men of different outlooks might mingle.

There were also many umbrella-owners present on the occasion who did not proffer their protection to those without cover. Hard to blame some. Their umbrellas were capable of covering one head only and surely it is better in the sight of God and man that one head be fully covered than two heads half drowned.

Others with outsize umbrellas held them grimly and firmly over their individual heads thereby convincing themselves that umbrellas were never made to be shared. Alas poor benighted fellows for they must miss the gratitude, the sense of benevolence and the camaraderie to be found under shared umbrellas. He is a fool indeed who fore-goes the opportunity of starting up a fresh acquaint-anceship, however brief, although it must be said here that there are those who rightfully feel that umbrellas should not be shared regardless of the downpour.

'Under no circumstances,' said a female relation of mine as she lowered her canopy after a shower 'would I let a man under my umbrella.'

When pressed for an explanation, she answered, 'because much always wants more.'

She had a point and females would do well to be watchful of those they leave under their umbrellas.

Still in a public place, under the public eye it is both safe and uplifting to share one's umbrella during a down-pour.

If you are young, the great advantage about sharing your umbrella is that you must move at the same pace as another while the rain is falling or the hail or the snow or the sleet or whatever and this is both a good beginning and a mighty discipline if one is to have a lasting and mean-ingful relationship later on in life. An umbrella shared is a conflict spared.

The Prophet

FEW CHARACTERS have appealed so much to readers of these essays as the Prophet Callaghan. He is dead now with over a score of years but his memory is fondly treasured by those fortunate enough to have known him. It's not because he was such a prodigious drinker of whiskey and porter that he is remembered; rather is it because he was such a dab hand at quoting from the scriptures and other apocryphal sources.

In fact this was why they nicknamed him the Prophet. His uncanny ability for coming up with apt quotes at just the right moment first came to light during the war years after he had cleaned out a pitch and toss school in Listowel's famous market sheds one rainy Sunday afternoon. With his winnings of several pounds, a small fortune in those days, he repaired with his friend Canavan to Mikey Dowling's public house in Market Street but was refused admittance on the grounds that it was after hours.

It was the same story in every pub from Pound Lane to the Customs' Gap. The forces of law and order, to wit the garda síochána were unusually active. The guards would explain later in their homely way that there had been letters to the barracks and that certain lawbreaking publicans had been mentioned in dispatches.

As Callaghan went homewards that night with his friend Canavan he remarked as he jingled the silver coins in his pockets 'What profiteth a man if he gain the whole world and he can't get a drink after hours?'

Another Sunday night the guards raided a pub in Upper Church Street. This pub was always regarded as being relatively safe because it was so near the garda barracks. Anyway Canavan and Callaghan were 'found on'. When asked by the sergeant to account for his presence on a licensed premises after hours Callaghan responded that he was only following the precepts of Saint Matthew.

'I don't follow,' said the sergeant.

'Ask and it shall be given,' Callaghan quoted, 'seek and ye shall find, knock and it shall be opened and lo and behold,' Canavan continued, 'I knocked and it was opened and that is the reason I am here.'

'All those,' said the sergeant, 'who live by the sword shall perish by the sword'.

'My God! My God!' said Callaghan, 'Why hast thou forsaken me?'

And it came to pass that after seven days Canavan and Callaghan anointed their outsides with soap and water and their insides with poitcheen and they came down from the mountain to the fleshpots of Listowel. In the town was a great circus and multitudes had gathered outside the doors of the taverns when the circus was over. Canavan and Callaghan were refused admission to all the hostelries so they journeyed to Ballybunion where they had not been before and they were graciously received and given credit and presented with cold plates for it so happened that there was an American wake in progress.

The days passed and Callaghan arrived at the Ballybunion publican's door with a bag of choice cabbage and a bucket of new potatoes.

'There's no need for that,' said the publican.

'Lo!' said Callaghan, 'I was hungry and ye gave me to eat. I was thirsty and ye gave me to drink. I was a stranger and ye took me in.'

Once at an American wake in Listowel Callaghan appeared to be exceedingly drunk. The man of the house told him he had enough when he proffered his cup for more drink.

'You're full to the brim,' said the woman of the house.

'I say to you,' quoth Callaghan, 'all the rivers run into

the sea and yet the sea is not full.'

He was a sick man the day after and the day after that again but the skies cleared when his friend Canavan arrived with the news that there was another American wake at McCarthy's of Finuge.

Quoth Callaghan 'As cold waters to a thirsty soul is good news from a far country'.

Speaking to One's Self

THE GREAT beneficial affect of speaking to one's self is that it is an act of intense privacy but when another listens in, as it were, it is not the same thing.

Recently in the city I heard a man shouting outside a hotel. He was ranting incoherently at passers-by but he was singling out nobody in particular. He was declaiming for all he was worth but what he was saying amounted to nonsense. There must have been a time, however, when he spoke sense instead of nonsense but because he could not hear himself in the city's tumult he had to raise his voice. The raising of his voice succeeded in startling many passers-by and this gave him a sense of power. He realised that the louder he spoke the more people became conscious of him. He could not know, poor, demented fellow, that they were merely aware of him and vaguely aware of him at that. To them he was just another drop in the ocean of oddities common to all cities.

Quite often people who speak to themselves in low tones are regarded as freaks despite the fact that each of us may find it necessary to speak to ourselves at certain times in life.

One might perhaps suggest that it would be more fitting to pray. Certainly prayer is good but self-address cannot be bettered in certain circumstances. Prayer, after all, is a recitation and what the human spirit sometimes needs is a boost which has been freshly baked in the oven of the noodle.

I remember once at Killarney Races to have backed a horse too heavily. My resources at the time were slender. When the horse came in well down the field I spoke to myself as follows: 'You danged nitwit, you ossified jackass that put every copper he had on an apology for a racecourse.'

Not content, however, with railing at myself I also kicked an empty tea chest which I refused to circumnavigate out of pure perverseness.

'There's no need to take it out on the poor box,' said a round-faced gentleman who stood nearby in his shirt sleeves. He happened to be the owner of several tea chests which he rented out to punters so that they might have an unimpaired view of the finish. I apologised to the man and would have offered him some small consolation in coinage but for losing all I had on the race. Afterwards I spoke exclusively to myself for several minutes until my sorrow and disappointment surrendered themselves to resignation.

Sometimes it is wise to talk to oneself when one is alone in dangerous territory as, for instance, an unlighted city street which may be peopled with gentlemen who survive by removing money from the pockets of perfect strangers and placing it in their own. One might address a question to oneself in a deep voice and respond to oneself in a high-pitched voice giving the impression to would-be muggers that they are likely to be contending with more than one victim.

In my youth I was friendly with a woman who used to speak to herself whilst coming to and going from her home. She also spoke to herself indoors but only when her husband was out. The reason she spoke so much to herself was that her husband was a taciturn fellow who seldom spoke but hummed, hawed and snorted all the time although never unkindly.

In the end she stopped speaking to him save when she would ask him questions like: 'Is it peas or beans you'll have?' or 'Do you want a hen egg or a duck egg?'

When she spoke to herself during his absence it was to defend him. She had a basic fear that she might grow to dislike him so what she did was to praise him to herself and she did it as though somebody else was doing the praising.

'Oh no dear me! He's not like that at all,' she would say as though somebody had insisted he was a blackguard.

'Sure wouldn't the creature give you the shirt off his back' she would carry on.

The pair lived happily over a long lifetime whereas certain other seemingly happy couples broke up and it could well be because they never spoke to themselves.

Word-Matching

I HAVE so often written about matchmaking in human terms that I have overlooked matchmaking in the wordy sense. I am not referring to poetry now or to colourful prose. What I am saying is that I have allowed certain words to run to seed by not matching them with others. In so doing I would allow them to fulfil their natural role which is to combine with other words to convey sentiments of delight and wonder, to relate feelings of love and tenderness, of joy and hope and the whole range of wonderful feelings which enrich the human experience.

Easy for you the gentle reader is sure to say. Your job is to wield words together. It's your trade and it's no great strain on you. This is not so at all. The mistake I have made all of my life was knitting words together which made commonsense and neglecting the joining of words which have no orthodox meaning.

I have been unfair to words for I believe that every word is entitled to the company of other words of its own choosing. Remember that the moment a word is pressed into service with a combination which has never been aired before it assumes a new status and yet it retains its individuality because it can be used again and again to form new and meaningful relationships.

I remember once to have been interviewed in the pub for a programme with some other men and women alleged to be artistically disposed. The interviewer, a bright fellow, decided to include a few laymen which is another name for a public house regular.

'What do you think of the situation?' he asked of our friend who was known to be somewhat illiterate and fond of reeling off cumbersome and unwieldy words at an extraordinary rate. He also spoke through his nose although many of his listeners would maintain that he spoke through a part of his anatomy further down. Be that as it may he answered as follows with a solemn mien as they say—'The situation,' said he, 'follows the confirmation of the glorification of the evaporation of the contamination in the continuation of the mortification of the hallucination of the entire nation and you could see a deterioration of the fortification with the assassination of the pasteurisation.'

I was amazed some weeks later as I listened to the programme on radio. Not a single word of our friend's extraordinary revelations had come across. They had been deliberately omitted. After they had been delivered in the pub there had been a sustained round of applause for this unprecedented bolderdash. The rest of us had said the usual clever things, the orthodox, the common and try as we might we rarely raised ourselves above the pedestrian.

When our friend had concluded on that drunken afternoon I felt elated. I may not have captured his outburst with total accuracy and I may even have left out a word or two but substantially I have reproduced what he said.

Bolderdash is a wonderful instrument. It can dissolve stuffiness in a matter of seconds. It disintegrates the desultory and confuses the canniest. Bolderdash delivered with the requisite pomp and authority will humble the wisest but you cannot have bolderdash without words and that is why I have come to enlist your aid in the manufacture of breathtaking, meaningless phrases, sentences and even paragraphs in the interests of fair play and common decency. I want you to blow the cobwebs off musty words by the simple expedient of introducing them to equally musty partners thereby giving a new lease of life individually and collectively.

I want you to disarm people who adopt no-nonsense attitudes by calefacting word combinations which will bewilder them but it is the employment of words that must principally concern us.

Go now into the world of light and bring with you a

retinue of under-used words of all shapes and sizes and do unto those words as you would have them do unto you for not by bread alone doth man live, nor by mustard but let your voice be raised with the next new moon.

Blow, Winds and Crack your Cheeks!

I LIKE uproarious days when the wind tries to blow the landscape away, when muck and puddles abound, when fresh floods chuckle under briars and hawthorn, when rivers are swollen and brown and the rain drives into my face, when the bare branches of tall trees gnash and lash and slates come crashing down. That's the time to be out of doors, to be uproarious too, to share the seasonal mood of the weather. That's my kind of day.

I like fine days too and I like frosty days and misty days but I'm a temperamental sort of fellow and I need a wind with force and power in it.

It's hard to define my craving for boisterous weather. I am not a boisterous fellow although you'll find me pulling my weight in a sing-song or shouting abuse at a poor-sighted referee but, generally speaking, I wish to live in peace and harmony with my fellow man.

I don't know what it is but a boisterous day full of wind and rain whets my appetite for life, summons me out of doors to participate in the celebrating tumult of the elements.

I think that in each of us there's a need at times to let oneself go, to have a bash at some unknown foe and I daresay that when the wind is raging around the skies and whipping through the woods and laneways the opportunity to take part in a ritual of natural violence cannot be resisted.

I have friends, however, who cannot bear loud winds or driving rain on the grounds that they deafen and intimidate.

I can also understand the apprehension of a man with a dubious roof where slates are loose or the thatch is crumbling. I share his fears but nevertheless the urge to participate in the devastating carnival outdoors dominates my thinking.

Often when the wind and rain bite into my face and restrain my advance I let go with a great roar and extend my arms in an effort to wrestle with the force which would hold me back. I jostle with gales and rainstorms, never allowing myself to retreat before them but always meeting them head on.

'Come on ye hoors!' I shout. 'Do yeer damnedest. Ye won't make me back down.'

They respond by blowing and puffing and drenching, by aggression and bluster. I know and they know that they could wipe me off the face of the earth if they so wished but like a good-natured mastiff with a tiny toy dog they are prepared to play the game with me for the fun of it.

There was a deceased relative of mine who sat for months expiring in a seat near the kitchen window. One day a great storm came and he asked to be let out into the middle of it.

'Now's the time! Now's the time!' he shouted. His daughter and her husband were mystified. How could they let him out and he bound by age and infirmity to his chair. What they could not understand was that he wanted to truly give vent to his ultimate feelings, he wanted to surrender his life to the elements and be borne aloft in the arms of the gale.

He needed to have his decline arrested and to be presented with the glorious gift of being disintegrated by the storm. He wanted nature to rejuvenate him before he surrendered to it. He wanted a final fling before decay. After all leaves are whipped aloft and tossed and gently borne before being deposited finally on the clay so why not he?

Those of us who love the clamour and challenge of wind and rain will sympathise with that old man who was nailed to his chair by his years. All he wanted in reality was the dignity of natural fragmentation and subsequent decay after nature had culled him as she did her other children.

Deer and salmon, wasp and woodcock are thus treated and rendered by the elements back into nature but not old men for laws ordain that they must die indoors.

Shakespeare in his late years would have understood the old man's feelings better than any for only a poet who braved the elements at their most potent could write for Lear as follows: —

> *Blow, winds and crack your cheeks!*
> *Rage! Blow!*
> *You cataracts and hurricanes spout!*
> *'Till you have drenched our steeples, drowned our*
> > *cocks!*

Let there be a gale then from Ballybunion-by-the-sea, a gale filled with infinitisemal spume tasting of brine and seaweed, sounding of seal barks and sea mews and then let the rain drive in behind in great blinding sheets and you'll be after making my day.

When Cats Die

BEWARE WHEN cats die! The cryptical observation came from a man named Joe the Pole who sat opposite me at the kitchen table where, with several others, we awaited our breakfast. The place was Northampton. The time was the early 1950s. As boarding houses go it wasn't a bad one. Meat and butter were still rationed but there was an abundance of fried bread, black puddings, eggs, beans and toast. Rashers were scarce but it was no hardship to make do with what was available.

Joe the Pole wasn't his real name. It was Josef Masawarawich. We called him Joe the Pole number one because there was another Josef with the surname Ritsapolopovitch so we called him Joe the Pole number two. They had both been in England since the beginning of the war.

'Beware when cats die!' It was the way Joe the Pole number one said it that advised us of the imminence of disaster. We had been waiting over twenty minutes for our beans and toast. In fact one of the company who couldn't wait any longer left the table muttering some uncalled-for obscenities. He was the same in public houses. If he wasn't noticed at once by the barman he would turn on his heel muttering the most diabolical threats ranging from castration to toe dismemberment.

Another of our party left and asked us to explain to the landlady that he dassn't be lite. 'I dassn't be lite,' he said fearfully. He was from the south-east of England and apparently his boss on the buses where he worked as a conductor hated all south-easterners, the reason being that his wife had run off with a waiter from Romney without warning of any kind.

Those of us who remained looked at our watches. We

had jobs. We could wait no longer. We exchanged looks. There was no sound from the kitchen.

Earlier the landlady had been called by her friend next door, a lady called Mrs Biggs. She had gone to the gate at the rear of the house on Mrs Biggs' insistence. She had not returned. Then from the distance came the sound of wailing. Had Mrs Biggs' husband been suddenly assumed into the hereafter! He was a wobbly blancmange of a fellow with a deep-seated allergy occasioned by the mention of work. Mrs Biggs also kept lodgers. Her husband came downstairs only when he was sure the lodgers had gone to work. When they returned for the evening meal he resumed his rightful place in the taproom of the local where he would intermittently criticise all Irish lodgers until closing time. We were Paddies and Shinners but worst of all we were gluttons and boozers. What harm but he could drink and eat the lot of us under a table. However let us return to the sound of the wailing.

It came nearer the kitchen slowly and pitifully. Finally it entered in the shape of Mrs Biggs. She paused, looked from one of us to another and, aided by our sympathetic faces, provided us with a virtuoso if hasty re-hash of all her previous pillalooing. She proceeded towards the head of the table where she stood silently, her hands partly covering her grief-stricken face, awaiting the remainder of the cortege which consisted of the next door neighbour from the other side and finally our landlady bearing the family tomcat in her arms. Instinctively we all stood, the Catholics amongst us fervently making the sign of the cross.

The cat was unmistakably dead, the last of his nine lives squandered in a reckless, daylight exercise which led him to blindly cross the road outside the lodgings in pursuit of a she-cat who had ogled him. He ran straight into the path of a passing taxi-cab. He momentarily forgot the age-old code of the cat kingdom; the day for dozing and the night for romancing.

The trio of disconsolate females stood silently, reproachful looks on their faces until we began to wonder how we had been remiss. It was Joe the Pole number one who rose to the occasion by deftly and noiselessly removing the ware from the table. I took responsibility for the condiments while Joe the Pole number two addressed himself to the cutlery. Mrs Biggs came forward and aided by the other neighbour ceremoniously folded the table cloth. Then and not till then did the landlady lay the cat upon the table.

Fondly she stroked his dark, glossy coat heaving great sighs all the while until it seemed that her very bosom, no longer able to contain the inexpressible grief, must surely collapse under the strain. We mumbled expressions of grief and departed. There had not been a single word about breakfast during the preliminary obsequies.

It was Shakespeare who said 'put not your trust in princes' as indeed we Irish might say 'put not your trust in cats'. We keep cats but we do not love cats the way the English do. We tolerate cats but we do not cosset cats. Consequently we do not grieve when cats die. We see the selfishness in cats, the treachery, the self-absorption, the cruelty. We are blind to the virtues. When our cats die they are promptly forgotten but the English remember their dead cats even at the going down of the sun and the coming up of the moon.

That evening when we returned for dinner there was none. Our landlady and Mrs Biggs sat in the kitchen with glasses in their hands. A gin bottle stood upon the table. There was no mention of dinner. It was all catstalk. They spoke between tears of his regular forays into the night world and of his final resting place in the little flower garden at the rear of the lodgings.

'Robin were a good cat,' Mrs Biggs shook her head.

"Im were good, Robin were,' the landlady concurred.

"Im with your old dad now,' said Mrs Biggs as she

helped them both to substantial refills of gin.

Those of us who trooped in from time to time trooped out again. In the sitting-room we held a council of war. Most of our lunches had been meagre but add to this the fact that we had no breakfasts and you will have gathered that there was mutiny in the air. There was again no breakfast the morning after but there was dinner that evening if dinner it could be called. There was, for the next week, a marked deterioration in the fare. One by one we left. A kitten appeared but if we were forced to wait until he grew into a cat and the return of normal conditions our constitutions must surely disintegrate. The majority defected to the perfidious Mrs Biggs. The rest of us took a flat. Our landlady died a month to the day after Robin. It had been a model lodgings. The transformation stunned us but it alerted us to the permanence of impermanence. How right Joe the Pole number one had been! Beware when cats die! Joe had been in England longer than any of us.

Pick your Moral

FOR OUR next story we will treat with the morals that are to be found in every story. Here is what I propose to do. I will relate the story to the best of my ability but I will not reveal the moral until the very end. That way you will have a chance to come up with your own moral. A moral a day, my grandmother used to say, keeps the devil at bay. So here's to morals. Let us embark upon our tale. Let us begin at the beginning and without further ado go straight through to the end.

Once upon a time a party of us were taken out to dinner by an elderly American monsignor who was related to us. He took us in two hired cars to Killarney. The Mons, as we called him, was a decent man. He liked public houses and he liked a bottle of wine with his meals. He always paid for the good reason that none of us, his relations, had money. No one had money in those days. People who had enough to eat were lucky. There were seven of us in the party, all related. To break our journey we had a drink in Tralee and for good measure another one in Farranfore. The Mons who came from a prosperous parish in California urged us not to spare him when the menus were submitted by a pair of friendly waitresses.

Although it's over forty years ago I still recall the winsome smiles of those two lovely girls but there was more to them than smiles. They were beautiful. They were courteous and efficient and they made us feel welcome.

Lunch began with an excellent soup. I've forgotten what kind but it tasted wonderful. This was followed by roast beef on the part of myself and the Mons and Jack. The others opted for sole, cutlets and omelette, a bit of a gamble at the time. Omelettes were teatime birds. It would have been unthinkable, for instance, for a man from the country-side to have an omelette for his dinner. Lunch was called dinner in those distant days. It still is in some isolated country places.

We wound up with rich desserts. Anything left on anybody's plate was quickly demolished by Jack. He was that kind of guy. He could eat anything, anywhere, anytime. He also consumed several pints of stout during the meal. All were charged up to the Monsignor's account.

'Drink up Jack,' was all that sainted man would say. He seemed to enjoy Jack's drinking more than his own. After each pint Jack would rub his hands together and shout at the waitresses who stood dutifully nearby. 'More porter' he would shout while they, for their part, would disappear instantly and return at once with a full pint of stout. With charming smiles they cleared away the ware and cutlery. At the end of the proceedings the Mons called for the bill.

It was served by the younger of the two as if it were the highlight of the lunch. Had I the money I would have been honoured to pay it. The priest looked at it and nodded approvingly. He paid out the exact amount and rose to depart but not before he thrust his hand into his trousers pocket and withdrew two half-crowns. He placed them under a solitary sugar bowl discreetly and strategically left behind. Then, led by the priest, a saintly man if ever there was one, we trooped out of the dining-room.

Jack remained behind, just a step or two behind. Then when he thought nobody was looking he lifted the sugar bowl and withdrew the five shillings. He put it in his pocket and shook his head, no doubt at the inexplicable eccentricities of elderly priests. At least that is precisely what he managed to convey to me.

The two waitresses had seen and I had seen but none of us had the courage to protest. It was a substantial sum of money at the time, worth about fifteen pounds today according to a maths' teacher who happened to be in the pub one night as I recalled the story. Jack did well in the world later on. He accumulated a vast fortune but alas he died young. There was no pain. His family went through his money like a fire through straw.

The moral here is that tips may vary in size but one precept always remains the same and that is that the horses that earn the oats don't always get them.

Dry Feet

FOR YEARS until recently I would be visited regularly by nose colds, head colds, varied influenzas from Asian to Californian and by numerous chills without name. I would suffer these unwelcome visitors in silence and between doctors and alcohol would struggle through to resume my rightful place among my neighbours and in the household. I was often left weak, debilitated and forlorn but last November to be exact I found a cure and since that time I have managed to successfully avoid all forms of nasal and bronchial beleaguerment.

Oddly enough it was a cure which was once passed on to a relation of mine by his mother. She happened to be on her deathbed at the time and when she beckoned him to bend for a final message he did so with alacrity. He was under the impression that she was about to reveal where her money was hidden. Alas for him the old lady was possessed of no earthly goods. What she unfolded to him would prove to be of greater value than any earthly possession but, of course, he had no way of knowing this at the time.

Her cracked, husky whispers penetrated to the farthest corners of the room and she managed to raise her grey head a few inches as she breathed forth her last message.

'Wash your feet,' she cackled, 'and you'll bury what's here.'

Although bitterly disappointed that there was no fortune forthcoming he nevertheless indulged his aged parent.

'I will mother. I will,' he vowed and all around heads nodded solemnly at this sign of filial deference. After the funeral in spite of the fact that he was three-quarters drunk he filled a basin of water and with the aid of a square of carbolic soap he proceeded to wash his feet. The operation took a full hour because those same feet had not been immersed in water for several years. Thinking that his promise had been filled he went to bed and slept the sleep of the just.

What his mother meant was that he should wash his feet on a regular basis. This he failed to do however and after a few short years he was carried off by pneumonia having failed to take off his wet boots on his return from the bog.

It may sound somewhat paradoxical but it is by washing our feet that we really come to dry them. Let me explain. Soft, moist or greasy feet are to the rest of the body what sinfulness is to the soul. Clammy feet, gluey feet and sappy feet are no better and it is to the dry foot that we must look if we are to expect our bodies as a whole to be healthy which brings us back to last November and to this man I chanced to meet in the residents' lounge of a well known Cork hotel. The bar had closed and we sat peacefully sipping our nightcaps before retiring to our respective chambers. I complained about a cold.

'I never get colds,' said he.

'I'm a martyr to colds,' said I.

'That's because you don't wash your feet,' said he.

'But I do wash my feet,' I replied without petulance.

'Of course you do,' he said, 'and so does every mother's son but do you wash your feet every day?'

I shook my head.

'I wash my feet every day,' said he, 'and then I pull on fresh socks and dry shoes. Sometimes if the weather is particularly wet I wash my feet twice a day and pull on fresh socks twice a day and dry shoes. You see I never throw shoes away.'

He wasn't in the least smug. He didn't have a cold. In fact he looked extremely healthy despite the fact that he looked an octogenarian at least.

Since that night I have washed my feet every day and sometimes twice a day. I have a wide selection of old shoes since I walk a lot. I have countless socks and if they don't all match that is the business of my feet and I. We are not, you must remember, entering for sock-matching competitions.

Since I started to wash my feet daily I have not received a single setback in chest or nose. My feet are always dry and the whole body stays dry with them. Ours is a united and a happy body because it stands on dry feet. Not on bread alone doth man live but on dry feet also. Try to remember that, you who are prey to the common cold.

Doing Nothing

'HE DOES nothing.' How often have we heard the expression and how often wrongly applied to many's the hardworking man.

A woman came into the pub the other day and said, 'I must tell you this.'

It transpired that she happened to be in a local boozer recently when a party of patrons from the extreme end of the parish arrived and made known their wants. Among them was a stranger, a small, polite, bespectacled woman from Scotland.

Apparently the group had visited my premises earlier in the day and also the previous night. On the first occasion they were looked after by my long suffering spouse and on the second by my daughter. The next thing you know they started to speak about the two visits to these oft-maligned precincts and it was at this juncture that the woman who visited me cocked her ears and devoted all her acoustic resources to the capture and retention of every last word. This turned out to be an easy job for it so happened that there was little to say.

'I didn't see the landlord in the bar,' said the kind little old lady from Caledonia, meaning me.

'Oh he's hardly ever in the bar,' said one of the local ladies.

'Not true, not true,' from one of the males in the company, both farmers and decent chaps to boot.

'Oh he does be in the bar all right,' said the other son of the soil, 'but he don't be serving. You'll nearly always see him on a high stool with a glass in his hand.'

'And the glass does not be empty either,' said his partner, 'although you'll see him once in a while collecting empties for his sins.'

'A good man to lower it,' said the other.

'None better,' said his pal. At this they both laughed. I laughed as well when I heard it. How's that Robbie Burns puts it:

> *Oh would some power*
> *the giftie gie us*
> *To see airselves as ithers*
> *see us.*

I was now being granted that rare power thanks to my caller but what a chastening experience it was, no accolade yet and none likely to come.

'Yes, yes,' said the Scotswoman with some irritation, 'but what does he do?'

'What does he do?' As one of my would-be biographers echoed the other in bewilderment they both looked to their womenfolk to provide the answer.

'He does nothing,' said the wife of the first while the wife of the second nodded in total agreement. So that was it. I did nothing and there I was all along thinking I was doing something.

The truth is that the kind people who said I was doing nothing firmly believed I was doing nothing for they looked upon the writing of plays, essays, stories and novels as a sort of harmless pastime and there are many who would agree with them.

Unfortunately there is a particular group of literary figures known as critics who take what writers produce seriously but these are of infinitesimal number and so they have little influence in the long run.

Then there was the night I was sitting outside the counter drinking pints with a few cronies when a man who was waiting for a drink asked if I did any work. He was an unpleasant fellow unlike most of the people who maintain I do nothing. My wife appeared and asked him his requirements but he was having none of it. 'I asked him first,' he said truculently.

'But,' said my wife, 'he's just a customer the same as you.'

This perplexed him but only for a little while.

'And a bloody good customer,' said one of my cronies.

'The best in the house,' said another kind soul. However it was all to no avail. The truculent visitor refused me the same rights which he took for granted himself. He went off in a huff vowing to go somewhere else where he would fare better.

Then the other night two young men from the town arrived and invested in two pints of beer. As my wife handed them out their change one asked her if John B. did anything.

'Oh,' said she, 'I look after the bar and he looks after the writing.' It all boils down to the same thing. Writing isn't working and I agree to some extent for I have always found it both relieving and relaxing when it's all over for the day or the night or whatever.

It's not the only work seen in this light. When I was younger a cousin of mine succeeded in securing a position as an insurance agent. The pay was small and the load was heavy 'but,' said his mother, 'you'll have nothing to do all day but drive around on your bike calling on people.'

Only this very day as recently as an hour ago my wife ran excitedly up the stairs and asked me if I had this particular piece finished.

'Not yet,' I replied.

'Good,' said she, 'because I have another piece for you.'

Apparently two able-bodied Laois men on their way to Tralee for the festival had just arrived on the premises and their first question was 'where is the boss?'

Now there's a good one. I'm not the boss. There had been a boss in their midst and they knew her not.

'He's working,' said she. At once they were impressed.

'Has he a job so?' asked one.

'The same as he always had,' said the missus, 'he's writing away upstairs.'

No longer were they impressed. They thought for a moment that I had been working and there was I all along doing nothing.

'Tis you does most of the work as far as I can see,' said the first of the Laois men.

There were times over the years when I might have believed that I was really doing nothing but then the money started to come in and I was reassured because nobody pays you for doing nothing. I remember some years ago I stayed up all night finishing a play. In the morning I happened to be seated in the bar reading a paper when a party of visitors arrived. The missus saw to their needs and then I heard one of them say as he pointed at me: 'Your man don't do a stroke.'

Here I am at this late stage of my life still doing nothing and highly successful at it. God be thanked and praised.